FROM THE PUBLISHER

More than three hundred years ago, the efforts of French author Charles Perrault helped define the fairy tale genre, taking what once had been an oral tradition and anchoring it in the written word. This Calla edition includes his graceful versions of Cinderilla, Sleeping Beauty, Little Red Riding-Hood, and seven other cherished favorites. To all of these Irish illustrator Harry Clarke injects his lush eccentricities: his work in color, pen & ink, and silhouette abounds, and allows these tales to operate on multiple levels of enjoyment.

Harry Clarke holds a unique place in the pantheon of outstanding book illustrators; clearly influenced by Aubrey Beardsley, he also looks ahead to the exotic imagery of 1960s psychedelia. His immersion in the world of book illustration was only partial, however, as he also turned his talented hand to stained-glass design and production, becoming Ireland's premier practitioner of this luminous art in the early twentieth century. Here twenty-four full-page illustrations and numerous vignettes demonstrate Clarke's mastery at infusing fantastic worlds with his darkly resonant vision.

THE FAIRY TALES OF CHARLES PERRAULT

CINDERILLA AND HER PRINCE

THE FAIRY TALES OF CHARLES PERRAULT

ILLUSTRATED BY HARRY CLARKE. WITH AN INTRODUCTION BY THOMAS BODKIN

CALLA EDITIONS

MINEOLA, NEW YORK

Bibliographical Note

The Fairy Tales of Charles Perrault, first published by Calla Editions in 2012, is
an unabridged reprint of the edition published by George G. Harrap & Co.
Ltd., London, in 1922.

International Standard Book Number

ISBN-13: 978-1-60660-027-6
ISBN-10: 1-60660-027-3

CALLA Editions
An imprint of Dover Publications, Inc.
www.callaeditions.com

Printed in China by C&C Offset Printing

CONTENTS

LIST OF ILLUSTRATIONS

FAIRY · TALES · OF · PERRAULT

INTRODUCTION

"Avec ardeur il aima les beaux arts."
Griselidis

*C*HARLES PERRAULT *must have been as charming a fellow as a man could meet. He was one of the best-liked personages of his own great age, and he has remained ever since a prime favourite of mankind. We are fortunate in knowing a great deal about his varied life, deriving our knowledge mainly from D'Alembert's history of the French Academy and from his own memoirs, which were written for his grandchildren, but not published till* *sixty-six years after his death. We should, I think, be more fortunate still if the memoirs had not ceased in mid-career, or if their author had permitted himself to write of his family affairs without reserve or restraint, in the approved manner of modern autobiography. We should like, for example, to know much more than we do about the wife and the two sons to whom he was so devoted.*

Perrault was born in Paris in 1628, the fifth son of Pierre Perrault, a prosperous parliamentary lawyer; and, at the age of nine, was sent to a day-school—the Collège de Beauvais. His father helped him with his lessons at home, as he himself, later on, was accustomed to help his own children. He can never have been a model schoolboy, though he was always first in his class, and he ended his school career prematurely by quarrelling with his master and bidding him a formal farewell.

The cause of this quarrel throws a bright light on Perrault's subsequent career. He refused to accept his teacher's philosophical tenets on the mere ground of their traditional authority. He claimed that novelty was in itself a merit, and on this they parted. He did not go alone. One of his friends, a boy called Beaurain, espoused his cause, and for the next three or four years the two read together, haphazard, in the Luxembourg Gardens. This plan of study had almost certainly a bad effect on Beaurain, for we hear no more of him. It certainly prevented Perrault from being a thorough scholar, though it made him a man of taste, a sincere independent, and an undaunted amateur.

In *1651* he took his degree at the University of Orléans, where degrees were given with scandalous readiness, payment of fees being the only essential preliminary. In the meantime he had walked the hospitals with some vague notion of following his brother Claude into the profession of medicine, and had played a small part as a theological controversialist in the quarrel then raging, about the nature of grace, between the Jesuits and the Jansenists. Having abandoned medicine and theology he got called to the Bar, practised for a while with distinct success, and coquetted with a notion of codifying the laws of the realm. The Bar proved too arid a profession to engage for long his attention; so he next sought and found a place in the office of another brother, Pierre, who was Chief Commissioner of Taxes in Paris. Here Perrault had little to do save to read at large in the excellent library which his brother had formed.

For want of further occupation he returned to the writing of verse, one of the chief pleasures of his boyhood. His first sustained literary effort had been a parody of the sixth book of the "Æneid"; which, perhaps fortunately for his reputation, was never published and has not survived. Beaurain and his brother Nicholas, a doctor of the Sorbonne, assisted him in this perpetration, and Claude made the pen-and-ink sketches with which it was illustrated. In the few years that had elapsed since the *writing of this burlesque Perrault had acquired more sense and taste, and his new poems—in particular the "Portrait d'Iris" and the "Dialogue entre l'Amour et l'Amitié"— were found charming by his contemporaries. They were issued anonymously, and Quinault, himself a poet of established reputation, used some of them to forward his suit with a young lady, allowing her to think that they were his own. Perrault, when told of Quinault's pretensions, deemed it necessary to disclose his authorship; but, on hearing of the use to which his work had been put, he gallantly remained in the background, forgave the fraud, and made a friend of the culprit.*

Architecture next engaged his attention, and in 1657 he designed a house at Viry for his brother and supervised its construction. Colbert approved so much of this performance that he employed him in the superintendence of the royal buildings and put him in special charge of Versailles, which was then in process of erection. Perrault flung himself with ardour into this work, though not to the exclusion of his other activities. He wrote odes in honour of the King; he planned designs for Gobelin tapestries and decorative paintings; he became a member of the select little Academy of Medals and Inscriptions which Colbert brought into being to devise suitable legends for the royal palaces and monuments; he encouraged musicians and fought the cause of Lulli; he joined with Claude in a successful effort to found the Academy of Science.

Claude Perrault had something of his brother's versatility and shared his love for architecture, and the two now became deeply interested in the various schemes which were mooted for the completion of the Louvre. Bernini was summoned by the King from Rome, and entrusted with the task; but the brothers Perrault intervened. Charles conceived the idea of the great east front and communicated it to Claude, who drew the plans and was commissioned to carry them out. The work was finished in 1671, and is still popularly known as Perrault's Colonnade.

In the same year Charles was elected to the Academy without any personal canvas on his part for the honour. His inaugural address was heard with such approval that he ventured to suggest that the inauguration of future members should be a public function. The suggestion was adopted, and these addresses became the most famous feature of the Academy's proceedings and are so to the present day. This was not his only service to the Academy, for he carried a motion to the effect that future elections should be by ballot; and invented and provided, at his own expense, a ballot-box which, though he does not describe it, was probably the model of those in use in all modern clubs and societies.

The novelty of his views did not always commend them to his brother 'Immortals.' Those expressed in his poem " Le Siècle de Louis XIV," which he read as an Academician of sixteen years' standing, initiated one of the most famous and lasting literary quarrels of the era. Perrault, in praising the writers of his own age, ventured to disparage some of the great authors of the ancient classics. Boileau lashed himself into a fury of opposition and hurled strident insults against the heretic. Racine, more adroit, pretended to think that the poem was a piece of ingenious irony. Most men of letters hastened to participate in the battle. No doubt Perrault's position was untenable, but he conducted his defence with perfect temper and much wit; and Boileau made himself not a little absurd by his violence and his obvious longing to display the extent of his learning. Perrault's case is finally stated in his four volumes, " Le Parallèle des Anciens et des Modernes," which were published in 1688-1696. He evidently took vastly more pride in this dull and now almost forgotten work than in the matchless stories which have made him famous for ever.

After twenty years in the service of Colbert, the sun of Perrault's fortunes passed its zenith. His brother, the Commissioner of Taxes, had a dispute with the Minister and was disgraced. Then Perrault got married to a young lady of whom we know nothing except that her marriage was the subject of some opposition from his powerful employer. In a matter of the sort Perrault, though a courtier, could be relied on to consider no wishes save those of his future wife and himself. Colbert's own influence with the King became shaky, and this affected his temper. So Perrault, then just fifty-five, slid quietly from his service in the year 1683.

INTRODUCTION

Before he went, he succeeded in frustrating a project for closing the Tuileries Gardens against the people of Paris and their children. Colbert proposed to reserve them to the royal use, but Perrault persuaded him to come there one day for a walk, showed him the citizens taking the air and playing with their, children; got the gardeners to testify that these privileges were never abused, and carried his point by declaring, finally, that "the King's pleasaunce was so spacious that there was room for all his children to walk there."

Sainte-Beuve, seventy years ago, pleaded that this service to the children of Paris should be commemorated by a statue of Perrault in the centre of the Tuileries. The statue has never been erected; and, to the present day, Paris, so plentifully provided with statues and pictures of the great men of France, has neither the one nor the other to show that she appreciates the genius of Perrault. Indeed, there is no statue of him in existence; and the only painting of him with which I am acquainted is a doubtful one hung far away in an obscure corner of the palace of Versailles.

The close of Perrault's official career marked the beginning of his period of greatest literary activity. In 1686 he published his long narrative poem "Saint Paulin Evesque de Nole" with "a Christian Epistle upon Penitence" and "an Ode to the Newly-converted," which he dedicated to Bossuet. Between the years 1688 and 1696 appeared the "Parallèle des Anciens et des Modernes" to which I have already referred. In 1693 he brought out his "Cabinet des Beaux Arts," beautifully illustrated by engravings, and containing a poem on painting which even Boileau condescended to admire. In 1694 he published his "Apologie des Femmes." He wrote two comedies—"L'Oublieux" in 1691, and "Les Fontanges." These were not printed till 1868. They added nothing to his reputation. Between 1691 and 1697 were composed the immortal "Histoires ou Contes du Temps Passé" and the "Contes en Vers." Toward the end of his life he busied himself with the "Éloges des Hommes Illustres du Siècle de Louis XIV." The first of these two stately volumes came out in 1696 and the second in 1700. They were illustrated by a hundred and two excellent engravings, including one, by Edelinck, of Perrault himself and another of his brother Claude. These biographies are written with kindly justice, and form a valuable contribution to the history of the reign of the Roi Soleil. I have not exhausted the list of Perrault's writings, but, to speak frankly, the rest are not worth mentioning.

He died, aged seventy-five, in 1703, deservedly admired and regretted by all who knew him. This was not strange. For he was clever, honest, courteous, and witty. He did his duty to his family, his employer, his friends, and to the public at large. In an age of great men, but also of great prejudices, he fought his own way to fame and fortune. He served all the arts, and practised most of them. Painters, writers, sculptors, musicians, and men of science all gladly made him free of their company. As a good Civil Servant he was no politician, and he showed no leaning whatever toward what was regarded in his time as the greatest of all professions—that of arms. These two deficiencies, if deficiencies they be, only endear him the more to us. Every one likes a man who deserves to enjoy life and does, in fact, enjoy it. Perrault was such a man. He was more. He was the cause of enjoyment to countless of his fellows, and his stories still promise enjoyment to countless others to come.

It is amazing to remember that Perrault was rather ashamed of his " Histoires ou Contes du Temps Passé "— perhaps better known as " Les Contes de ma Mère l'Oye," or " Mother Goose's Tales," from the rough print which was inserted as a frontispiece to the first collected edition in 1697. He would not even publish them in his own name. They were declared to be by P. Darmancour, Perrault's young son. In order that the secret might be well kept, Perrault abandoned his usual publisher, Coignard, and went to Barbin. The stories had previously appeared from time to time, anonymously, in Moetjens' little magazine the " Recueil," which was published from The Hague. " La Belle au Bois Dormant " (" Sleeping Beauty ") was the first : and in rapid succession followed " Le Petit Chaperon Rouge " (" Red Riding-Hood "), " Le Maistre Chat, ou le Chat Botté " (" Puss in Boots "), " Les Fées " (" The Fairy "), " Cendrillon, ou la Petite Pantoufle de Verre " (" Cinderella "), " Riquet à la Houppe" ("Riquet of the Tuft"), and "Le Petit Poucet" ("Tom Thumb").

Perrault was not so shy in admitting the authorship of his three verse stories—"Griselidis," "Les Souhaits Ridicules," and "Peau d'Asne." The first appeared, anonymously it is true, in 1691; but, when it came to be reprinted with "Les Souhaits Ridicules" and "Peau d'Asne" in 1695, they were entrusted to the firm of Coignard and described as being by "Mr Perrault, de l'Academie Françoise." La Fontaine had made a fashion of this sort of exercise.

It would not be fair to assume that P. Darmancour had no connection whatever with the composition of the stories which bore his name. The best of Perrault's critics, Paul de St Victor and Andrew Lang among others, see in the book a marvellous collaboration of crabbed age and youth. The boy, probably, gathered the stories from his nurse and brought them to his father, who touched them up, and toned them down, and wrote them out. Paul Lacroix, in his fine edition of 1886, goes as far as to attribute the entire authorship of the prose tales to Perrault's son. He deferred, however, to universal usage when he entitled his volume "Les Contes en prose de Charles Perrault."

"Les Contes du Temps Passé" had an immediate success. Imitators sprung up at once by the dozen, and still persist; but none of them has ever rivalled, much less surpassed, the inimitable originals. Every few years *a new and sumptuous edition appears in France. The best are probably those by Paul Lacroix and André le Fèvre.*

The stories soon crossed the Channel; and a translation "by Mr Samber, printed for J. Pote" was advertised in the "Monthly Chronicle" of 1729. "Mr Samber" was presumably one Robert Samber of New Inn, who translated other tales from the French, for Edmond Curl the bookseller, about this time. No copy of the first edition of his Perrault is known to exist. Yet it won a wide popularity, as is shown by the fact that there was a seventh edition published in 1795, for J. Rivington, a bookseller, of Pearl Street, New York.

No English translation of Perrault's fairy tales has attained unquestioned literary pre-eminence. So the publishers of the present book have thought it best to use Samber's translation, which has a special interest of its own in being almost contemporary with the original. The text has been thoroughly revised and corrected by Mr J. E. Mansion, who has purged it of many errors without detracting from its old-fashioned quality. To Mr Mansion also is due the credit for the translation of the "Les Souhaits Ridicules" and for the adaptation of "Peau d'Asne." "Griselidis" is excluded from this book for two good reasons; firstly, because it is an admitted borrowing by Perrault from Boccaccio; secondly, because it is not a 'fairy' tale in the true sense of the word.

It is, perhaps, unnecessary for me to add anything about

19

Mr Clarke's illustrations. Many of the readers of this book will be already familiar with his work. Besides, I always feel that it is an impertinence to describe pictures in their presence. Mr Clarke's speak for themselves. They speak for Perrault too. It is seldom, indeed, that an illustrator enters so thoroughly into the spirit of his text. The grace, delicacy, urbanity, tenderness, and humour which went to the making of Perrault's stories must, it seems, have also gone in somewhat similar proportions to the making of these delightful drawings. I am sure that they would have given pleasure to Perrault himself.

THOMAS BODKIN

Little Red Riding-Hood

Little ▫ Red ▫ Riding-Hood

ONCE upon a time, there lived in a certain village, a little country girl, the prettiest creature was ever seen. Her mother was excessively fond of her; and her grand-mother doated on her much more. This good woman got made for her a little red riding-hood; which became the girl so extremely well, that every body called her Little Red Riding-Hood.

One day, her mother, having made some girdle-cakes, said to her:

"Go, my dear, and see how thy grand-mamma does, for I hear she has been very ill, carry her a girdle-cake, and this little pot of butter."

Little Red Riding-Hood set out immediately to go to her grand-mother, who lived in another village. As she was going thro' the wood, she met with Gaffer Wolf, who had a very great mind to eat her up, but he durst not, because of some faggot-makers hard by in the forest.

He asked her whither she was going. The poor child, who did not know that it was dangerous to stay and hear a Wolf talk, said to him:

"I am going to see my grand-mamma, and carry her a girdle-cake, and a little pot of butter, from my mamma."

"Does she live far off?" said the Wolf.

"Oh! ay," answered Little Red Riding-Hood, "it is

beyond that mill you see there, at the first house in the village."

"Well," said the Wolf, "and I'll go and see her too: I'll go this way, and you go that, and we shall see who will be there soonest."

The Wolf began to run as fast as he could, taking the nearest way; and the little girl went by that farthest about, diverting herself in gathering nuts, running after butterflies, and making nosegays of such little flowers as she met with. The Wolf was not long before he got to the old woman's house: he knocked at the door, *tap*, *tap*.

"Who's there?"

"Your grand-child, Little Red Riding-Hood," replied the Wolf, counterfeiting her voice, "who has brought you a girdle-cake, and a little pot of butter, sent you by mamma."

The good grand-mother, who was in bed, because she found herself somewhat ill, cry'd out:

"Pull the peg, and the bolt will fall."

The Wolf pull'd the peg, and the door opened, and then presently he fell upon the good woman, and ate her up in a moment; for it was above three days that he had not touched a bit. He then shut the door, and went into the grand-mother's bed, expecting Little Red Riding-Hood, who came some time afterwards, and knock'd at the door, *tap*, *tap*.

"Who's there?"

Little Red Riding-Hood, hearing the big voice of the

"HE ASKED HER WHITHER SHE WAS GOING"

Wolf, was at first afraid ; but believing her grand-mother had got a cold, and was hoarse, answered :

"'Tis your grand-child, Little Red Riding-Hood, who has brought you a girdle-cake, and a little pot of butter, mamma sends you."

The Wolf cried out to her, softening his voice as much as he could, "Pull the peg, and the bolt will fall."

Little Red Riding-Hood pulled the peg, and the door opened. The Wolf seeing her come in, said to her, hiding himself under the bedclothes :

"Put the cake, and the little pot of butter upon the bread-bin, and come and lye down with me."

Little Red Riding-Hood undressed herself, and went into bed ; where, being greatly amazed to see how her grand-mother looked in her night-cloaths, she said to her :

"Grand-mamma, what great arms you have got!"

"That is the better to hug thee, my dear."

"Grand-mamma, what great legs you have got!"

"That is to run the better, my child."

"Grand-mamma, what great ears you have got!"

"That is to hear the better, my child."

"Grand-mamma, what great eyes you have got!"

"It is to see the better, my child."

"Grand-mamma, what great teeth you have got!"

"That is to eat thee up."

And, saying these words, this wicked Wolf fell upon poor Little Red Riding-Hood, and ate her all up.

25

The Moral

From this short story easy we discern
What conduct all young people ought to learn.
But above all, young, growing misses fair,
Whose orient rosy blooms begin t'appear :
Who, beauties in the fragrant spring of age,
With pretty airs young hearts are apt t'engage.
Ill do they listen to all sorts of tongues,
Since some inchant and lure like Syrens' songs.
No wonder therefore 'tis, if over-power'd,
So many of them has the Wolf devour'd.
The Wolf, I say, for Wolves too sure there are
Of every sort, and every character.
Some of them mild and gentle-humour'd be,
Of noise and gall, and rancour wholly free ;
Who tame, familiar, full of complaisance
Ogle and leer, languish, cajole and glance ;
With luring tongues, and language wond'rous sweet,
Follow young ladies as they walk the street,
Ev'n to their very houses, nay, bedside,
And, artful, tho' their true designs they hide ;
Yet ah ! these simpering Wolves ! Who does not see
Most dangerous of Wolves indeed they be ?

The Fairy

"'WHAT IS THIS I SEE?' SAID HER MOTHER"
(*page* 30)

· The · Fairy ·

THERE was, once upon a time, a widow, who had two daughters. The eldest was so much like her in the face and humour, that whoever looked upon the daughter saw the mother. They were both so disagreeable, and so proud, that there was no living with them. The youngest, who was the very picture of her father, for courtesy and sweetness of temper, was withal one of the most beautiful girls ever seen. As people naturally love their own likeness, this mother even doated on her eldest daughter, and at the same time had a horrible aversion for the youngest. She made her eat in the kitchen, and work continually.

Among other things, this poor child was forced twice a day to draw water above a mile and a half off the house, and bring home a pitcher full of it. One day, as she was at this fountain, there came to her a poor woman, who begged of her to let her drink.

"O ay, with all my heart, Goody," said this pretty maid; and rinsing immediately the pitcher, she took up some water from the clearest place of the fountain, and gave it to her, holding up the pitcher all the while, that she might drink the easier.

The good woman having drank, said to her:

"You are so very pretty, my dear, so good and so mannerly, that I cannot help giving you a gift" (for this was a Fairy, who had taken the form of a poor country-woman, to

29

see how far the civility and good manners of this pretty girl would go). "I will give you for gift," continued the Fairy, "that at every word you speak, there shall come out of your mouth either a flower, or a jewel."

When this pretty girl came home, her mother scolded at her for staying so long at the fountain.

"I beg your pardon, mamma," said the poor girl, "for not making more haste," and, in speaking these words, there came out of her mouth two roses, two pearls, and two diamonds.

"What is this I see?" said her mother quite astonished, "I think I see pearls and diamonds come out of the girl's mouth! How happens this, child?" (This was the first time she ever called her child.)

The poor creature told her frankly all the matter, not without dropping out infinite numbers of diamonds.

"In good faith," cried the mother, "I must send my child thither. Come hither, Fanny, look what comes out of thy sister's mouth when she speaks! Would'st not thou be glad, my dear, to have the same gift given to thee? Thou hast nothing else to do but go and draw water out of the fountain, and when a certain poor woman asks thee to let her drink, to give it her very civilly."

"It would be a very fine sight indeed," said this ill-bred minx, "to see me go draw water!"

"You shall go, hussey," said the mother, "and this minute."

" 'AM I COME HITHER TO SERVE YOU WITH WATER, PRAY?' "

So away she went, but grumbling all the way, taking with her the best silver tankard in the house.

She was no sooner at the fountain, than she saw coming out of the wood a lady most gloriously dressed, who came up to her, and asked to drink. This was, you must know, the very Fairy who appeared to her sister, but had now taken the air and dress of a princess, to see how far this girl's rudeness would go.

"Am I come hither," said the proud, saucy slut, "to serve you with water, pray? I suppose the silver tankard was brought purely for your ladyship, was it? However, you may drink out of it, if you have a fancy."

"You are not over and above mannerly," answered the Fairy, without putting herself in a passion. "Well then, since you have so little breeding, and are so disobliging, I give you for gift, that at every word you speak there shall come out of your mouth a snake or a toad."

So soon as her mother saw her coming, she cried out: "Well, daughter?"

"Well, mother?" answered the pert hussey, throwing out of her mouth two vipers and two toads.

"O mercy!" cried the mother, "what is it I see! O, it is that wretch her sister who has occasioned all this; but she shall pay for it"; and immediately she ran to beat her. The poor child fled away from her and went to hide herself in the forest, not far from thence.

The King's son, then on his return from hunting, met

her, and seeing her so very pretty, asked her what she did there alone, and why she cried.

"Alas! sir, my mamma has turned me out of doors."

The King's son, who saw five or six pearls, and as many diamonds, come out of her mouth, desired her to tell him how that happened. She thereupon told him the whole story; and so the King's son fell in love with her; and, considering with himself that such a gift was worth more than any marriage-portion whatsoever in another, conducted her to the palace of the King his father, and there married her.

As for her sister, she made herself so much hated that her own mother turned her off; and the miserable wretch, having wandered about a good while without finding anybody to take her in, went to a corner in the wood and there died.

The Moral

Money and jewels still, we find,
Stamp strong impressions on the mind.
But sweet discourse more potent riches yields;
Of higher value is the pow'r it wields.

Another

Civil behaviour costs indeed some pains,
Requires of complaisance some little share;
But soon or late its due reward it gains,
And meets it often when we're not aware.

Blue Beard

" 'WHAT, IS NOT THE KEY OF MY CLOSET AMONG THE REST?' "

(*page* 40)

▫ Blue ▫ Beard ▫

THERE was a man who had fine houses, both in town and country, a deal of silver and gold plate, embroidered furniture, and coaches gilded all over with gold. But this man had the misfortune to have a blue beard, which made him so frightfully ugly, that all the women and girls ran away from him.

One of his neighbours, a lady of quality, had two daughters who were perfect beauties. He desired of her one of them in marriage, leaving to her the choice which of the two she would bestow upon him. They would neither of them have him, and each made the other welcome of him, being not able to bear the thought of marrying a man who had a blue beard. And what besides gave them disgust and aversion, was his having already been married to several wives, and no-body ever knew what became of them.

Blue Beard, to engage their affection, took them, with the lady their mother, and three or four ladies of their acquaintance, with other young people of the neighbourhood, to one of his country seats, where they stayed a whole week. There was nothing then to be seen but parties of pleasure, hunting, fishing, dancing, mirth and feasting. No-body went to bed, but all passed the night in playing tricks upon each other. In short, every thing succeeded so well, that the youngest daughter began to think the master of the house not to have a beard so very blue, and that he was a mighty civil gentleman. As soon as they returned home, the marriage was concluded.

About a month afterwards Blue Beard told his wife that he was obliged to take a country journey for six weeks at least, about affairs of very great consequence, desiring her to divert herself in his absence, to send for her friends and acquaintances, to carry them into the country, if she pleased, and to make good cheer wherever she was.

" Here," said he, " are the keys of the two great wardrobes, wherein I have my best furniture ; these are of my silver and gold plate, which is not every day in use ; these open my strong boxes, which hold my money, both gold and silver ; these my caskets of jewels ; and this is the master-key to all my apartments. But for this little one here, it is the key of the closet at the end of the great gallery on the ground floor. Open them all ; go into all and every one of them ; except that little closet which I forbid you, and forbid it in such a manner that, if you happen to open it, there will be no bounds to my just anger and resentment."

She promised to observe, very exactly, whatever he had ordered ; when he, after having embraced her, got into his coach and proceeded on his journey.

Her neighbours and good friends did not stay to be sent for by the newmarried lady, so great was their impatience to see all the rich furniture of her house, not daring to come while her husband was there, because of his blue beard which frightened them. They ran thro' all the rooms, closets, and

"THIS MAN HAD THE MISFORTUNE TO HAVE A BLUE BEARD"

wardrobes, which were all so rich and fine, that they seemed
to surpass one another.

After that, they went up into the two great rooms, where
were the best and richest furniture ; they could not sufficiently
admire the number and beauty of the tapestry, beds, couches,
cabinets, stands, tables, and looking-glasses in which you
might see yourself from head to foot ; some of them were
framed with glass, others with silver, plain and gilded, the
finest and most magnificent which were ever seen. They
ceased not to extol and envy the happiness of their friend,
who in the mean time no way diverted herself in looking upon
all these rich things, because of the impatience she had to go
and open the closet of the ground floor. She was so much
pressed by her curiosity, that, without considering that it was
very uncivil to leave her company, she went down a little
back-stair-case, and with such excessive haste, that she had
twice or thrice like to have broken her neck.

Being come to the closet door, she made a stop for some
time, thinking upon her husband's orders, and considering
what unhappiness might attend her if she was disobedient ;
but the temptation was so strong she could not overcome it.
She took then the little key, and opened it trembling ; but
could not at first see any thing plainly, because the windows
were shut. After some moments she began to perceive that
the floor was all covered over with clotted blood, in which
were reflected the bodies of several dead women ranged against
the walls : these were all the wives whom Blue Beard had

married and murdered one after another. She was like to have died for fear, and the key, which she pulled out of the lock, fell out of her hand.

After having somewhat recovered her senses, she took up the key, locked the door, and went up stairs into her chamber to recover herself; but she could not, so much was she frightened. Having observed that the key of the closet was stained with blood, she tried two or three times to wipe it off, but the blood would not come off; in vain did she wash it, and even rub it with soap and sand, the blood still remained, for the key was a Fairy, and she could never make it quite clean; when the blood was gone off from one side, it came again on the other.

Blue Beard returned from his journey the same evening, and said, he had received letters upon the road, informing him that the affair he went about was ended to his advantage. His wife did all she could to convince him she was extremely glad of his speedy return. Next morning he asked her for the keys, which she gave him, but with such a trembling hand, that he easily guessed what had happened.

"What," said he, "is not the key of my closet among the rest?"

"I must certainly," answered she, "have left it above upon the table."

"Fail not," said Blue Beard, "to bring it me presently."

After putting him off several times, she was forced to

bring him the key. Blue Beard, having very attentively considered it, said to his wife:

"How comes this blood upon the key?"

"I do not know," cried the poor woman, paler than death.

"You do not know," replied Blue Beard; "I very well know, you were resolved to go into the closet, were you not? Mighty well, Madam; you shall go in, and take your place among the ladies you saw there."

Upon this she threw herself at her husband's feet, and begged his pardon with all the signs of a true repentance for her disobedience. She would have melted a rock, so beautiful and sorrowful was she; but Blue Beard had a heart harder than any rock.

"You must die, Madam," said he, "and that presently."

"Since I must die," answered she, looking upon him with her eyes all bathed in tears, "give me some little time to say my prayers."

"I give you," replied Blue Beard, "half a quarter of an hour, but not one moment more."

When she was alone, she called out to her sister, and said to her:

"Sister Anne" (for that was her name), "go up I beg you, upon the top of the tower, and look if my brothers are not coming; they promised me that they would come to-day, and if you see them, give them a sign to make haste."

Her sister Anne went up upon the top of the tower, and the poor afflicted wife cried out from time to time, "Anne, sister Anne, do you see any one coming?"

And sister Anne said:

"I see nothing but the sun, which makes a dust, and the grass growing green."

In the mean while Blue Beard, holding a great scimitar in his hand, cried out as loud as he could bawl to his wife:

"Come down instantly, or I shall come up to you."

"One moment longer, if you please," said his wife, and then she cried out very softly:

"Anne, sister Anne, dost thou see any body coming?"

And sister Anne answered:

"I see nothing but the sun, which makes a dust, and the grass growing green."

"Come down quickly," cried Blue Beard, "or I will come up to you."

"I am coming," answered his wife; and then she cried:

"Anne, sister Anne, dost thou see any one coming?"

"I see," replied sister Anne, "a great dust that comes this way."

"Are they my brothers?"

"Alas! no, my dear sister, I see a flock of sheep."

"Will you not come down?" cried Blue Beard.

"One moment longer," said his wife, and then she cried out:

"Anne, sister Anne, dost thou see nobody coming?"

"I see," said she, "two horsemen coming, but they are yet a great way off."

"God be praised," she cried presently, "they are my brothers; I am beckoning to them, as well as I can, for them to make haste."

Then Blue Beard bawled out so loud, that he made the whole house tremble. The distressed wife came down, and threw herself at his feet, all in tears, with her hair about her shoulders.

"Nought will avail," said Blue Beard, "you must die"; then, taking hold of her hair with one hand, and lifting up his scimitar with the other, he was going to take off her head.

The poor lady turning about to him, and looking at him with dying eyes, desired him to afford her one little moment to recollect herself.

"No, no," said he, "recommend thyself to God," and was just ready to strike.

At this very instant there was such a loud knocking at the gate, that Blue Beard made a sudden stop. The gate was opened, and presently entered two horsemen, who drawing their swords, ran directly to Blue Beard. He knew them to be his wife's brothers, one a dragoon, the other a musqueteer; so that he ran away immediately to save himself; but the two brothers pursued so close, that they overtook him before he could get to the steps of the porch, when they ran their swords thro' his body and left him dead. The poor wife was almost as dead as her husband, and had not strength enough to rise and welcome her brothers.

Blue Beard had no heirs, and so his wife became mistress of all his estate. She made use of one part of it to marry her sister Anne to a young gentleman who had loved her a long while; another part to buy captains' commissions for her brothers; and the rest to marry herself to a very worthy gentleman, who made her forget the ill time she had passed with Blue Beard.

The Moral

O curiosity, thou mortal bane!
Spite of thy charms, thou causest often pain
And sore regret, of which we daily find
A thousand instances attend mankind:
For thou—O may it not displease the fair—
A fleeting pleasure art, but lasting care.
And always proves, alas! too dear the prize,
Which, in the moment of possession, dies.

Another

A very little share of common sense,
And knowledge of the world, will soon evince
That this a story is of time long pass'd;
No husbands now such panic terrors cast;
Nor weakly, with a vain despotic hand,
Imperious, what's impossible, command:
And be they discontented, or the fire
Of wicked jealousy their hearts inspire,
They softly sing; and of whatever hue
Their beards may chance to be, or black, or blue,
Grizeld, or russet, it is hard to say
Which of the two, the man or wife, bears sway.

The Sleeping Beauty
in the Wood

"AT THIS VERY INSTANT THE YOUNG FAIRY CAME OUT FROM BEHIND THE HANGINGS"

(page 50)

· The · Sleeping · Beauty · · in · the · Wood ·

THERE were formerly a King and a Queen, who were so sorry that they had no children, so sorry that it cannot be expressed. They went to all the waters in the world; vows, pilgrimages, all ways were tried and all to no purpose. At last, however, the Queen proved with child, and was brought to bed of a daughter. There was a very fine christening; and the Princess had for her god-mothers all the Fairies they could find in the whole kingdom (they found seven), that every one of them might give her a gift, as was the custom of Fairies in those days, and that by this means the Princess might have all the perfections imaginable.

After the ceremonies of the christening were over, all the company returned to the King's palace, where was prepared a great feast for the Fairies. There was placed before every one of them a magnificent cover with a case of massive gold, wherein were a spoon, knife and fork, all of pure gold set with diamonds and rubies. But as they were all sitting down at table, they saw come into the hall a very old Fairy whom they had not invited, because it was above fifty years since she had been out of a certain tower, and she was believed to be either dead or inchanted. The King ordered her a cover, but could not furnish her with a case of gold as the others, because they had seven only made for the seven Fairies. The old Fairy fancied she was slighted, and muttered some threat between her teeth. One of the young Fairies, who sat by her, over-heard how she grumbled; and judging that she might give the little Princess some unlucky gift, went, as soon as they rose from the table, and hid herself behind the hangings, that she might speak last, and repair, as much as possible she could, the evil which the old Fairy might intend.

In the mean while all the Fairies began to give their gifts to the Princess. The youngest gave her for gift, that she should be the most beautiful person in the world; the next, that she should have the wit of an angel; the third, that she should have a wonderful grace in every thing she did; the fourth, that she should dance perfectly well; the fifth, that she should sing like a nightingale; and the sixth, that she should play upon all kinds of music to the utmost perfection.

The old Fairy's turn coming next, with a head shaking more with spite than age, she said, that the Princess should have her hand pierced with a spindle, and die of the wound. This terrible gift made the whole company tremble, and every body fell a-crying.

At this very instant the young Fairy came out from behind the hangings, and spake these words aloud:

"Be reassured, O King and Queen; your daughter shall not die of this disaster: it is true, I have no power to undo intirely what my elder has done. The Princess shall indeed pierce her hand with a spindle; but instead of dying, she shall only fall into a profound sleep, which shall last a hundred years; at the expiration of which a king's son shall come and awake her."

The King, to avoid the misfortune foretold by the old Fairy, caused immediately proclamations to be made, whereby every-body was forbidden, on pain of death, to spin with a distaff and spindle or to have so much as any spindle in their houses.

About fifteen or sixteen years after, the King and Queen being gone to one of their houses of pleasure, the young Princess happened one day to divert herself running up and down the palace; when going up from one apartment to another, she came into a little room on the top of a tower, where a good old woman, alone, was spinning with her spindle. This good woman had never heard of the King's proclamation against spindles.

"What are you doing there, Goody?" said the Princess.

"I am spinning, my pretty child," said the old woman, who did not know who she was.

"Ha!" said the Princess, "this is very pretty; how do you do it? Give it to me, that I may see if I can do so." She had no sooner taken the spindle into her hand, than, whether being very hasty at it, somewhat unhandy, or that the decree of the Fairy had so ordained it, it ran into her hand, and she fell down in a swoon.

The good old woman not knowing very well what to do in this affair, cried out for help. People came in from every quarter in great numbers; they threw water upon the Princess's face, unlaced her, struck her on the palms of her hands, and rubbed her temples with Hungary-water; but nothing would bring her to herself.

And now the King, who came up at the noise, bethought himself of the prediction of the Fairies, and judging very well that this must necessarily come to pass, since the Fairies had said it, caused the Princess to be carried into the finest apartment in his palace, and to be laid upon a bed all embroidered with gold and silver. One would have taken her for an angel, she was so very beautiful; for her swooning away had not diminished one bit of her complexion; her cheeks were carnation, and her lips like coral; indeed her eyes were shut, but she was heard to breathe softly, which satisfied those about her that she was not dead. The King commanded that they should not disturb her, but let her sleep quietly till her hour of awakening was come.

The good Fairy, who had saved her life by condemning her to sleep a hundred years, was in the kingdom of Matakin, twelve thousand leagues off, when this accident befell the Princess; but she was instantly informed of it by a little dwarf, who had boots of seven leagues, that is, boots with which he could tread over seven leagues of ground at one stride. The Fairy came away immediately, and she arrived, about an hour after, in a fiery chariot, drawn by dragons. The King handed her out of the chariot, and she approved every thing he had done; but, as she had a very great foresight, she thought, when the Princess should awake, she might not know what to do with herself, being all alone in this old palace; and this was what she did: She touched with her wand every thing in the palace (except the King and the Queen), governesses, maids of honour, ladies of the bed-chamber, gentlemen, officers, stewards, cooks, under-cooks, scullions, guards, with their beef-eaters, pages, footmen; she likewise touched all the horses which were in the stables, as well as their grooms, the great dogs in the outward court, and pretty little Mopsey too, the Princess's little spaniel-bitch, which lay by her on the bed.

Immediately upon her touching them, they all fell asleep, that they might not awake before their mistress, and that they might be ready to wait upon her when she wanted them. The very spits at the fire, as full as they could hold of partridges and pheasants, did fall asleep, and the fire likewise. All this was done in a moment. Fairies are not long in doing their business.

And now the King and the Queen, having kissed their dear child without waking her, went out of the palace, and put forth a proclamation, that nobody should dare to come near it. This, however, was not necessary; for, in a quarter of an hour's time, there grew up, all round about the park, such a vast number of trees, great and small, bushes and brambles, twining one within another, that neither man nor beast could pass thro'; so that nothing could be seen but the very top of the towers of the palace; and that too, not unless it was a good way off. Nobody doubted but the Fairy gave herein a sample of her art, that the Princess, while she continued sleeping, might have nothing to fear from any curious people.

When a hundred years were gone and past, the son of the King then reigning, and who was of another family from that of the sleeping Princess, being gone a-hunting on that side of the country, asked, what were those towers which he saw in the middle of a great thick wood? Every one answered according as they had heard; some said that it was a ruinous old castle, haunted by spirits; others, that all the sorcerers and witches of the country kept there their sabbath, or nights meeting. The common opinion was that an Ogre[1] lived there, and that he carried thither all the little children he could catch, that he might eat them up at his leisure, without any-body's being able to follow him, as having himself, only, the power to pass thro' the wood.

The Prince was at a stand, not knowing what to believe, when a very aged countryman spake to him thus: " May it please your Royal Highness, it is now above fifty years since I heard my father, who had heard my grandfather, say that there then was in this castle, a Princess, the most beautiful was ever seen; that she must sleep there a hundred years, and should be awaked by a king's son; for whom she was

---

[1] OGRE is a giant, with long teeth and claws, with a raw head and bloody-bones, who runs away with naughty little boys and girls, and eats them up. [Note by the translator.]

THE PRINCE ENQUIRES OF THE AGED COUNTRYMAN

reserved." The young Prince was all on fire at these words, believing, without a moment's doubt, that he could put an end to this rare adventure; and pushed on by love and honour resolved that moment to look into it.

Scarce had he advanced towards the wood, when all the great trees, the bushes and brambles, gave way of themselves to let him pass thro'; he walked up to the castle which he saw at the end of a large avenue which he went into; and what a little surprised him was, that he saw none of his people could follow him, because the trees closed again, as soon as he had pass'd thro' them. However, he did not cease from continuing his way; a young and amorous Prince is always valiant. He came into a spacious outward court, where everything he saw might have frozen up the most fearless person with horror. There reigned over all a most frightful silence; the image of death everywhere shewed itself, and there was nothing to be seen but stretched out bodies of men and animals, all seeming to be dead. He, however, very well knew, by the ruby faces and pimpled noses of the beef-eaters, that they were only asleep; and their goblets, wherein still remained some drops of wine, shewed plainly, that they fell asleep in their cups.

He then crossed a court paved with marble, went up the stairs, and came into the guard-chamber, where the guards were standing in their ranks, with their muskets upon their shoulders, and snoring as loud as they could. After that he went through several rooms full of gentlemen and ladies, all asleep, some standing, others sitting. At last he came into a chamber all gilded with gold, where he saw, upon a bed, the curtains of which were all open, the finest sight was ever beheld: a Princess, who appeared to be about fifteen or sixteen years of age, and whose bright, and in a manner resplendent beauty, had somewhat in it divine. He approached with trembling and admiration, and fell down before her upon his knees.

And now, as the inchantment was at an end, the Princess awaked, and looking on him with eyes more tender than the first view might seem to admit of: "Is it you, my Prince," said she to him, "you have tarried long."

The Prince, charmed with these words, and much more with the manner in which they were spoken, knew not how to shew his joy and gratitude; he assured her, that he loved her better than he did himself; his discourse was not well connected, but it pleased her all the more; little eloquence, a great deal of love. He was more at a loss than she, and we need not wonder at it; she had time to think on what to say to him; for it is very probable (though history mentions nothing of it) that the good Fairy, during so long a sleep, had entertained her with pleasant dreams. In short, when they talked four hours together, they said not half what they had to say.

In the mean while, all the palace awaked; every one thought upon their particular business; and as all of them were not in love, they were ready to die for hunger; the chief lady of honour, being as sharp set as other folks, grew very

"HE SAW, UPON A BED, THE FINEST SIGHT WAS EVER BEHELD"

impatient, and told the Princess aloud, That supper was served up. The Prince helped the Princess to rise, she was entirely dressed, and very magnificently, but his Royal Highness took care not to tell her that she was dressed like his great grand-mother, and had a point-band peeping over a high collar; she looked not a bit the less beautiful and charming for all that.

They went into the great hall of looking-glasses, where they supped, and were served by the Princess's officers; the violins and hautboys played old tunes, but very excellent, tho' it was now above a hundred years since they had been played; and after supper, without losing any time, the lord almoner married them in the chapel of the castle, and the chief lady of honour drew the curtains. They had but very little sleep; the Princess had no occasion, and the Prince left her next morning to return into the city, where his father must needs have been anxious on his account. The Prince told him that he lost his way in the forest, as he was hunting, and that he had lain at the cottage of a collier, who gave him cheese and brown bread.

The King his father, who was of an easy disposition, believed him; but his mother could not be persuaded this was true; and seeing that he went almost every day a-hunting, and that he always had some excuse ready when he had laid out three or four nights together, she no longer doubted he had some little amour, for he lived with the Princess above two whole years, and had by her two children, the eldest of which, who was a daughter, was named Aurora, and the youngest, who was a son, they called Day, because he was even handsomer and more beautiful than his sister.

The Queen said more than once to her son, in order to bring him to speak freely to her, that a young man must e'en take his pleasure; but he never dared to trust her with his secret; he feared her, tho' he loved her; for she was of the race of the Ogres, and the King would never have married her, had it not been for her vast riches; it was even whispered about the court, that she had Ogreish inclinations, and that, whenever she saw little children passing by, she had all the difficulty in the world to refrain from falling upon them. And so the Prince would never tell her one word.

But when the King was dead, which happened about two years afterwards; and he saw himself lord and master, he openly declared his marriage; and he went in great ceremony to fetch his Queen from the castle. They made a magnificent entry into the capital city, she riding between her two children.

Some time after, the King went to make war with the Emperor Cantalabutte, his neighbour. He left the government of the kingdom to the Queen his mother, and earnestly recommended to her care his wife and children. He was like to be at war all the summer, and as soon as he departed, the Queen-mother sent her daughter-in-law and her children to a country-house among the woods, that she might with the more ease gratify her horrible longing.

" 'I WILL HAVE IT SO,' REPLIED THE QUEEN, 'AND WILL EAT HER WITH A SAUCE ROBERT' "

Some few days afterwards she went thither herself, and said to her clerk of the kitchen :

"I have a mind to eat little Aurora for my dinner to morrow."

"Ah! Madam," cried the clerk of the kitchen.

"I will have it so," replied the Queen (and this she spake in the tone of an Ogress, who had a strong desire to eat fresh meat), "and will eat her with a Sauce Robert."[1]

The poor man knowing very well that he must not play tricks with Ogresses, took his great knife and went up into little Aurora's chamber. She was then four years old, and came up to him jumping and laughing, to take him about the neck, and ask him for some sugar-candy. Upon which he began to weep, the great knife fell out of his hand, and he went into the back-yard, and killed a little lamb, and dressed it with such good sauce, that his mistress assured him she had never eaten anything so good in her life. He had at the same time taken up little Aurora, and carried her to his wife, to conceal her in the lodging he had at the end of the court yard.

About eight days afterwards, the wicked Queen said to the clerk of the kitchen :

"I will sup upon little Day."

He answered not a word, being resolved to cheat her, as he had done before. He went to find out little Day, and saw

---

[1] This is a French sauce, made with onions shredded and boiled tender in butter, to which is added vinegar, mustard, salt, pepper, and a little wine. [Note by the translator.]

him with a little foil in his hand, with which he was fencing with a great monkey; the child being then only three years of age. He took him up in his arms, and carried him to his wife, that she might conceal him in her chamber along with his sister, and in the room of little Day cooked up a young kid very tender, which the Ogress found to be wonderfully good.

This was hitherto all mighty well: but one evening this wicked Queen said to her clerk of the kitchen:

"I will eat the Queen with the same sauce I had with her children."

It was now that the poor clerk of the kitchen despaired of being able to deceive her. The young Queen was turned of twenty, not reckoning the hundred years she had been asleep: her skin was somewhat tough, tho' very fair and white; and how to find in the yard a beast so firm, was what puzzled him. He took then a resolution, that he might save his own life, to cut the Queen's throat; and going up into her chamber, with intent to do it at once, he put himself into as great a fury as he could possibly, and came into the young Queen's room with his dagger in his hand. He would not, however, surprise her, but told her, with a great deal of respect, the orders he had received from the Queen-mother.

"Do it, do it," said she stretching out her neck, "execute your orders, and then I shall go and see my children, my poor children, whom I so much and so tenderly loved," for she thought them dead ever since they had been taken away without her knowledge.

"No, no, Madam," cried the poor clerk of the kitchen, all in tears, "you shall not die, and yet you shall see your children again; but it must be in my lodgings, where I have concealed them, and I shall deceive the Queen once more, by giving her in your stead a young hind."

Upon this he forthwith conducted her to his chamber; where leaving her to embrace her children, and cry along with them, he went and dressed a hind, which the Queen had for her supper, and devoured it with the same appetite, as if it had been the young Queen. Exceedingly was she delighted with her cruelty, and she had invented a story to tell the King, at his return, how ravenous wolves had eaten up the Queen his wife, and her two children.

One evening, as she was, according to her custom, rambling round about the courts and yards of the palace, to see if she could smell any fresh meat, she heard, in a ground-room little Day crying, for his mamma was going to whip him, because he had been naughty; and she heard, at the same time, little Aurora begging pardon for her brother.

The Ogress presently knew the voice of the Queen and her children, and being quite mad that she had been thus deceived, she commanded next morning, by break of day (with a most horrible voice, which made every body tremble) that they should bring into the middle of the great court a large tub, which she caused to be filled with toads, vipers,

63

snakes, and all sorts of serpents, in order to have thrown into it the Queen and her children, the clerk of the kitchen, his wife and maid; all whom she had given orders should be brought thither with their hands tied behind them.

They were brought out accordingly, and the executioners were just going to throw them into the tub, when the King (who was not so soon expected) entered the court on horseback (for he came post) and asked, with the utmost astonishment, what was the meaning of that horrible spectacle? No one dared to tell him; when the Ogress, all inraged to see what had happened, threw herself head-foremost into the tub, and was instantly devoured by the ugly creatures she had ordered to be thrown into it for others. The King could not but be very sorry, for she was his mother; but he soon comforted himself with his beautiful wife, and his pretty children.

The Moral

To get as prize a husband rich and gay,
Of humour sweet, with many years to stay,
Is natural enough, 'tis true;
To wait for him a hundred years,
And all that while asleep, appears
A thing entirely new.
Now at this time of day,
Not one of all the sex we see
Doth sleep with such profound tranquillity:
But yet this Fable seems to let us know
That very often Hymen's blisses sweet,
Altho' some tedious obstacles they meet,
Are not less happy for approaching slow.
'Tis nature's way that ladies fair
Should yearn conjugal joys to share;
And so I've not the heart to preach
A moral that's beyond their reach.

The Master Cat; or,
Puss in Boots

▫ The ▫ Master ▫ Cat ▫
▫ or ▫ Puss ▫ in ▫ Boots ▫

THERE was a miller, who left no more estate to the three sons he had, than his Mill, his Ass, and his Cat. The partition was soon made. Neither the scrivener nor attorney were sent for. They would soon have eaten up all the poor patrimony. The eldest had the Mill, the second the Ass, and the youngest nothing but the Cat.

The poor young fellow was quite comfortless at having so poor a lot.

"My brothers," said he, "may get their living handsomely enough, by joining their stocks together; but for my part, when I have eaten up my Cat, and made me a muff of his skin, I must die with hunger."

The Cat, who heard all this, but made as if he did not, said to him with a grave and serious air:

"Do not thus afflict yourself, my good master; you have only to give me a bag, and get a pair of boots made for me, that I may scamper thro' the dirt and the brambles, and you shall see that you have not so bad a portion of me as you imagine."

Tho' the Cat's master did not build very much upon what he said, he had however often seen him play a great many cunning tricks to catch rats and mice; as when he used to hang by the heels, or hide himself in the meal, and make as if he were dead; so that he did not altogether despair of his affording him some help in his miserable condition.

When the Cat had what he asked for, he booted himself very gallantly; and putting his bag about his neck, he held the strings of it in his two fore paws, and went into a warren where was great abundance of rabbits. He put bran and sow-thistle into his bag, and stretching himself out at length, as if he had been dead, he waited for some young rabbit, not yet acquainted with the deceits of the world, to come and rummage his bag for what he had put into it.

Scarce was he lain down, but he had what he wanted; a rash and foolish young rabbit jumped into his bag, and Monsieur Puss, immediately drawing close the strings, took and killed him without pity. Proud of his prey, he went with it to the palace, and asked to speak with his Majesty. He was shewed up stairs into the King's apartment, and, making a low reverence, said to him:

"I have brought you, sir, a rabbit of the warren which my noble lord the Marquis of Carabas" (for that was the title which Puss was pleased to give his master) "has commanded me to present to your Majesty from him."

"Tell thy master," said the King, "that I thank him, and that he does me a great deal of pleasure."

Another time he went and hid himself among some standing corn, holding still his bag open; and when a brace of partridges ran into it, he drew the strings, and so caught them both. He went and made a present of these to the

King, as he had done before of the rabbit which he took in the warren. The King in like manner received the partridges with great pleasure, and ordered him some money to drink.

The Cat continued for two or three months, thus to carry his Majesty, from time to time, game of his master's taking. One day in particular, when he knew for certain that the King was to take the air, along the river side, with his daughter, the most beautiful Princess in the world, he said to his master:

"If you will follow my advice, your fortune is made; you have nothing else to do, but go and wash yourself in the river, in that part I shall shew you, and leave the rest to me."

The Marquis of Carabas did what the Cat advised him to, without knowing why or wherefore.

While he was washing, the King passed by, and the Cat began to cry out, as loud as he could:

"Help, help, my lord Marquis of Carabas is drowning."

At this noise the King put his head out of his coach-window, and finding it was the Cat who had so often brought him such good game, he commanded his guards to run immediately to the assistance of his lordship the Marquis of Carabas.

While they were drawing the poor Marquis out of the river, the Cat came up to the coach, and told the King that while his master was washing, there came by some rogues, who went off with his clothes, tho' he had cried out "Thieves, thieves," several times, as loud as he could. This cunning

Cat had hidden them under a great stone. The King immediately commanded the officers of his wardrobe to run and fetch one of his best suits for the lord Marquis of Carabas.

The King received him with great kindness, and as the fine clothes he had given him extremely set off his good mien (for he was well made, and very handsome in his person), the King's daughter took a secret inclination to him, and the Marquis of Carabas had no sooner cast two or three respectful and somewhat tender glances, but she fell in love with him to distraction. The King would needs have him come into his coach, and take part of the airing. The Cat, quite over-joyed to see his project begin to succeed, marched on before, and meeting with some countrymen, who were mowing a meadow, he said to them :

"Good people, you who are mowing, if you do not tell the King, that the meadow you mow belongs to my lord Marquis of Carabas, you shall be chopped as small as mince-meat."

The King did not fail asking of the mowers, to whom the meadow they were mowing belonged.

"To my lord Marquis of Carabas," answered they all together ; for the Cat's threats had made them terribly afraid.

"Truly a fine estate," said the King to the Marquis of Carabas.

"You see, sir," said the Marquis, "this is a meadow which never fails to yield a plentiful harvest every year."

The Master Cat, who still went on before, met with some reapers, and said to them:

"Good people, you who are reaping, if you do not tell the King that all this corn belongs to the Marquis of Carabas, you shall be chopped as small as mince-meat."

The King, who passed by a moment after, would needs know to whom all that corn, which he then saw, did belong. "To my lord Marquis of Carabas," replied the reapers; and the King again congratulated the Marquis.

The Master Cat, who went always before, said the same words to all he met; and the King was astonished at the vast estates of my lord Marquis of Carabas.

Monsieur Puss came at last to a stately castle, the master of which was an Ogre, the richest had ever been known; for all the lands which the King had then gone over belonged to this castle. The Cat, who had taken care to inform himself who this Ogre was, and what he could do, asked to speak with him, saying, he could not pass so near his castle, without having the honour of paying his respects to him.

The Ogre received him as civilly as an Ogre could do, and made him sit down.

"I have been assured," said the Cat, "that you have the gift of being able to change yourself into all sorts of creatures you have a mind to; you can, for example, transform yourself into a lion, or elephant, and the like."

"This is true," answered the Ogre very briskly, "and to convince you, you shall see me now become a lion."

Puss was so sadly terrified at the sight of a lion so near him, that he immediately got into the gutter, not without abundance of trouble and danger, because of his boots, which were ill-suited for walking upon the tiles. A little while after, when Puss saw that the Ogre had resumed his natural form, he came down, and owned he had been very much frightened.

"I have been moreover informed," said the Cat, "but I know not how to believe it, that you have also the power to take on you the shape of the smallest animals; for example, to change yourself into a rat or a mouse; but I must own to you, I take this to be impossible."

"Impossible?" cried the Ogre, "you shall see that presently," and at the same time changed into a mouse, and began to run about the floor.

Puss no sooner perceived this, but he fell upon him, and eat him up.

Meanwhile the King, who saw, as he passed, this fine castle of the Ogre's, had a mind to go into it. Puss, who heard the noise of his Majesty's coach running over the drawbridge, ran out and said to the King:

"Your Majesty is welcome to this castle of my lord Marquis of Carabas."

"What! my lord Marquis?" cried the King, "and does this castle also belong to you? There can be nothing finer than this court, and all the stately buildings which surround it; let us go into it, if you please."

The Marquis gave his hand to the Princess, and followed

"THE MARQUIS GAVE HIS HAND TO THE PRINCESS, AND FOLLOWED THE KING,
WHO WENT UP FIRST"

the King, who went up first. They passed into a spacious hall, where they found a magnificent collation which the Ogre had prepared for his friends, who were that very day to visit him, but dared not to enter knowing the King was there. His Majesty was perfectly charmed with the good qualities of my lord Marquis of Carabas, as was his daughter who was fallen violently in love with him ; and seeing the vast estate he possessed, said to him, after having drank five or six glasses :

"It will be owing to yourself only, my lord Marquis, if you are not my son-in-law."

The Marquis making several low bows, accepted the honour which his Majesty conferred upon him, and forthwith, that very same day, married the Princess.

Puss became a great lord, and never ran after mice any more, but only for his diversion.

The Moral

How advantageous it may be,
By long descent of pedigree,
  T'enjoy a great estate,
Yet knowledge how to act, we see,
Join'd with consummate industry,
  (Nor wonder ye thereat)
Doth often prove a greater boon,
As should be to young people known.

Another

If the son of a miller so soon gains the heart
Of a beautiful princess, and makes her impart
Sweet languishing glances, eyes melting for love,
It must be remark'd of fine clothes how they move,
And that youth, a good face, a good air, with good
  mien,
Are not always indifferent mediums to win
The love of the fair, and gently inspire
The flames of sweet passion, and tender desire.

Cinderilla; or,
The Little Glass Slipper

"AWAY SHE DROVE, SCARCE ABLE TO CONTAIN HERSELF FOR JOY"

(page 84)

▫ Cinderilla ▫ or ▫ The ▫ Little ▫ Glass ▫ Slipper ▫

ONCE there was a gentleman who married, for his second wife, the proudest and most haughty woman that was ever seen. She had, by a former husband, two daughters of her own humour and they were indeed exactly like her in all things. He had likewise, by another wife, a young daughter, but of unparalleled goodness and sweetness of temper, which she took from her mother, who was the best creature in the world.

No sooner were the ceremonies of the wedding over, but the stepmother began to shew herself in her colours. She could not bear the good qualities of this pretty girl; and the less, because they made her own daughters appear the more odious. She employed her in the meanest work of the house; she scoured the dishes, tables, &c. and rubbed Madam's chamber, and those of Misses, her daughters; she lay up in a sorry garret, upon a wretched straw-bed, while her sisters lay in fine rooms, with floors all inlaid, upon beds of the very newest fashion, and where they had looking-glasses so large, that they might see themselves at their full length, from head to foot.

The poor girl bore all patiently, and dared not tell her father, who would have rattled her off; for his wife governed him intirely. When she had done her work, she used to go into the chimney-corner, and sit down among cinders and ashes, which made her commonly be called Cinder-breech; but the youngest, who was not so rude and uncivil as the eldest, called her Cinderilla. However, Cinderilla, notwithstanding her mean apparel, was a hundred times handsomer than her sisters, tho' they were always dressed very richly.

It happened that the King's son gave a ball, and invited all persons of fashion to it. Our young misses were also invited; for they cut a very grand figure among the quality. They were mightily delighted at this invitation, and wonderfully busy in chusing out such gowns, petticoats, and headclothes as might best become them. This was a new trouble to Cinderilla; for it was she who ironed her sisters' linen, and plaited their ruffles; they talked all day long of nothing but how they should be dressed. "For my part," said the eldest, "I will wear my red velvet suit, with French trimming." "And I," said the youngest, "shall only have my usual petticoat; but then, to make amends for that, I will put on my gold-flowered manteau, and my diamond stomacher, which is far from being the most ordinary one in the world." They sent for the best tire-woman they could get, to make up their head-dresses, and adjust their double-pinners,[1] and they had their red brushes, and patches from the fashionable maker.

Cinderilla was likewise called up to them to be consulted in all these matters, for she had excellent notions, and advised

---

[1] 'Pinners' were coifs with two long side-flaps pinned on. 'Double-pinners'—with two side-flaps on each side—accurately translates the French *cornettes à deux rangs*.

"ANY ONE BUT CINDERILLA WOULD HAVE DRESSED THEIR HEADS AWRY"

them always for the best, nay and offered her service to dress their heads, which they were very willing she should do. As she was doing this, they said to her:

"Cinderilla, would you not be glad to go to the ball?"

"Ah!" said she, "you only jeer at me; it is not for such as I am to go thither."

"Thou art in the right of it," replied they, "it would make the people laugh to see a Cinder-breech at a ball."

Any one but Cinderilla would have dressed their heads awry, but she was very good, and dressed them perfectly well. They were almost two days without eating, so much they were transported with joy; they broke above a dozen of laces in trying to be laced up close, that they might have a fine slender shape, and they were continually at their looking-glass. At last the happy day came; they went to Court, and Cinderilla followed them with her eyes as long as she could, and when she had lost sight of them she fell a-crying.

Her godmother, who saw her all in tears, asked her what was the matter.

"I wish I could——, I wish I could—;" she was not able to speak the rest, being interrupted by her tears and sobbing.

This godmother of hers, who was a Fairy, said to her:

"Thou wishest thou couldest go to the ball, is it not so?"

"Y—es," cried Cinderilla, with a great sigh.

"Well," said her godmother, "be but a good girl, and I will contrive that thou shalt go." Then she took her into her chamber, and said to her:

"Run into the garden, and bring me a pumpkin."

Cinderilla went immediately to gather the finest she could get, and brought it to her godmother, not being able to imagine how this pumpkin could make her go to the ball. Her godmother scooped out all the inside of it, leaving nothing but the rind; which done, she struck it with her wand, and the pumpkin was instantly turned into a fine coach, gilded all over with gold.

She then went to look into her mouse-trap, where she found six mice all alive, and ordered Cinderilla to lift up a little the trap-door, when giving each mouse, as it went out, a little tap with her wand, the mouse was at that moment turned into a fair horse, which altogether made a very fine set of six horses of a beautiful mouse-coloured dapple-grey.

Being at a loss for a coachman, "I will go and see," says Cinderilla, "if there be never a rat in the rat-trap, that we may make a coachman of him."

"Thou art in the right," replied her godmother; "go and look."

Cinderilla brought the trap to her, and in it there were three huge rats. The Fairy made choice of one of the three, which had the largest beard, and, having touched him with her wand, he was turned into a fat jolly coachman, who had the smartest whiskers eyes ever beheld.

After that, she said to her:

"Go again into the garden, and you will find six lizards behind the watering pot; bring them to me."

She had no sooner done so, but her godmother turned them into six footmen, who skipped up immediately behind the coach, with their liveries all bedaubed with gold and silver, and clung as close behind it, as if they had done nothing else their whole lives. The Fairy then said to Cinderilla:

"Well, you see here an equipage fit to go to the ball with; are you not pleased with it?"

"O yes," cried she, "but must I go thither as I am, in these poison nasty rags?"

Her godmother only just touched her with her wand, and, at the same instant, her clothes were turned into cloth of gold and silver, all beset with jewels. This done she gave her a pair of glass-slippers,[1] the prettiest in the whole world.

Being thus decked out, she got up into her coach; but her godmother, above all things, commanded her not to stay till after midnight, telling her, at the same time, that if she stayed at the ball one moment longer, her coach would be a pumpkin again, her horses mice, her coachman a rat, her footmen lizards, and her clothes become just as they were before.

---

[1] In Perrault's tale: *pantoufles de verre.* There is no doubt that in the medieval versions of this ancient tale Cinderilla was given *pantoufles de vair*—i.e., of a grey, or grey and white, fur, the exact nature of which has been a matter of controversy, but which was probably a grey squirrel. Long before the seventeenth century the word *vair* had passed out of use, except as a heraldic term, and had ceased to convey any meaning to the people. Thus the *pantoufles de vair* of the fairy tale became, in the oral tradition, the homonymous *pantoufles de verre*, or glass slippers, a delightful improvement on the earlier version.

She promised her godmother, she would not fail of leaving the ball before midnight; and then away she drove, scarce able to contain herself for joy. The King's son, who was told that a great Princess, whom no-body knew, was come, ran out to receive her; he gave her his hand as she alighted out of the coach, and led her into the hall, among all the company. There was immediately a profound silence, they left off dancing, and the violins ceased to play, so attentive was every one to contemplate the singular beauty of this unknown new comer. Nothing was then heard but a confused noise of,

"Ha! how handsome she is! Ha! how handsome she is!"

The King himself, old as he was, could not help ogling her, and telling the Queen softly, "that it was a long time since he had seen so beautiful and lovely a creature." All the ladies were busied in considering her clothes and head-dress, that they might have some made next day after the same pattern, provided they could meet with such fine materials, and as able hands to make them.

The King's son conducted her to the most honourable seat, and afterwards took her out to dance with him: she danced so very gracefully, that they all more and more admired her. A fine collation was served up, whereof the young Prince ate not a morsel, so intently was he busied in gazing on her. She went and sat down by her sisters, shewing them a thousand civilities, giving them part of the oranges and citrons which the Prince had presented her with; which very much surprised them, for they did not know her.

While Cinderilla was thus amusing her sisters, she heard the clock strike eleven and three quarters, whereupon she immediately made a curtesy to the company, and hasted away as fast as she could.

Being got home, she ran to seek out her godmother, and after having thanked her, she said, "she could not but heartily wish she might go next day to the ball, because the King's son had desired her." As she was eagerly telling her godmother whatever had passed at the ball, her two sisters knocked at the door which Cinderilla ran and opened.

"How long you have stayed," cried she, gaping, rubbing her eyes, and stretching herself as if she had been just awaked out of her sleep; she had not, however, any manner of inclination to sleep since they went from home.

"If thou hadst been at the ball," said one of her sisters, "thou wouldst not have been tired with it; there came thither the finest Princess, the most beautiful ever was seen with mortal eyes; she shewed us a thousand civilities, and gave us oranges and citrons." Cinderilla was transported with joy; she asked them the name of that Princess; but they told her they did not know it; and that the King's son was very anxious to learn it, and would give all the world to know who she was. At this Cinderilla, smiling, replied:

"She must then be very beautiful indeed; Lord! how happy have you been; could not I see her? Ah! dear Miss

Charlotte, do lend me your yellow suit of cloaths which you wear every day!"

"Ay, to be sure!" cried Miss Charlotte, "lend my cloaths to such a dirty Cinder-breech as thou art; who's the fool then?"

Cinderilla, indeed, expected some such answer, and was very glad of the refusal; for she would have been sadly put to it, if her sister had lent her what she asked for jestingly.

The next day the two sisters were at the ball, and so was Cinderilla, but dressed more magnificently than before. The King's son was always by her, and never ceased his compliments and amorous speeches to her; to whom all this was so far from being tiresome, that she quite forgot what her godmother had recommended to her, so that she, at last, counted the clock striking twelve, when she took it to be no more than eleven; she then rose up, and fled as nimble as a deer.

The Prince followed, but could not overtake her. She left behind one of her glass slippers, which the Prince took up most carefully. She got home, but quite out of breath, without coach or footmen, and in her nasty old cloaths, having nothing left her of all her finery, but one of the little slippers, fellow to that she dropped. The guards at the palace gate were asked if they had not seen a Princess go out; who said, they had seen no-body go out, but a young girl, very meanly dressed, and who had more the air of a poor country wench, than a gentle-woman.

"SHE LEFT BEHIND ONE OF HER GLASS SLIPPERS, WHICH THE PRINCE TOOK UP MOST CAREFULLY"

When the two sisters returned from the ball, Cinderilla asked them if they had been well diverted, and if the fine lady had been there. They told her, Yes, but that she hurried away immediately when it struck twelve, and with so much haste, that she dropped one of her little glass slippers, the prettiest in the world, and which the King's son had taken up; that he had done nothing but look at it during all the latter part of the ball, and that most certainly he was very much in love with the beautiful person who owned the little slipper.

What they said was very true; for a few days after, the King's son caused it to be proclaimed by sound of trumpet, that he would marry her whose foot this slipper would just fit. They whom he employed began to try it on upon the Princesses, then the duchesses, and all the Court, but in vain. It was brought to the two sisters, who did all they possibly could to thrust their feet into the slipper, but they could not effect it.

Cinderilla, who saw all this, and knew her slipper, said to them laughing:

" Let me see if it will not fit me ? "

Her sisters burst out a-laughing, and began to banter her. The gentleman who was sent to try the slipper, looked earnestly at Cinderilla, and finding her very handsome, said it was but just that she should try, and that he had orders to let every one make tryal. He invited Cinderilla to sit down, and putting the slipper to her foot, he found it went on very easily, and fitted her, as if it had been made of wax. The astonishment her two sisters were in was excessively great, but still abundantly greater, when Cinderilla pulled out of her pocket the other slipper, and put it on her foot. Thereupon, in came her godmother, who having touched, with her wand, Cinderilla's cloaths, made them richer and more magnificent than any of those she had before.

And now her two sisters found her to be that fine beautiful lady whom they had seen at the ball. They threw themselves at her feet, to beg pardon for all the ill treatment they had made her undergo. Cinderilla took them up, and as she embraced them, cried that she forgave them with all her heart, and desired them always to love her.

She was conducted to the young Prince, dressed as she was; he thought her more charming than ever, and, a few days after, married her.

Cinderilla, who was no less good than beautiful, gave her two sisters lodgings in the palace, and that very same day matched them with two great lords of the court.

The Moral

Beauty's to the sex a treasure,
Still admir'd beyond all measure,
And never yet was any known,
By still admiring, weary grown.
But that rare quality call'd grace,
Exceeds, by far, a handsome face;
Its lasting charms surpass the other,
And this rich gift her kind godmother
Bestow'd on Cinderilla fair,
Whom she instructed with such care.
She gave to her such graceful mien,
That she, thereby, became a queen.
For thus (may ever truth prevail)
We draw our moral from this tale.
This quality, fair ladies, know
Prevails much more (you'll find it so)
T'ingage and captivate a heart,
Than a fine head dress'd up with art.
The fairies' gift of greatest worth
Is grace of bearing, not high birth;
Without this gift we'll miss the prize;
Possession gives us wings to rise.

Another

A great advantage 'tis, no doubt, to man,
To have wit, courage, birth, good sense, and brain,
And other such-like qualities, which we
Receiv'd from heaven's kind hand, and destiny.
But none of these rich graces from above,
To your advancement in the world will prove
If godmothers and sires you disobey,
Or 'gainst their strict advice too long you stay.

Riquet with the Tuft

Riquet ▫ with ▫ the ▫ Tuft

THERE was, once upon a time, a Queen, who was brought to bed of a son, so hideously ugly, that it was long disputed, whether he had human form. A Fairy, who was at his birth, affirmed, he would be very lovable for all that, since he should be indowed with abundance of wit. She even added, that it would be in his power, by virtue of a gift she had just then given him, to bestow on the person he most loved as much wit as he pleased. All this somewhat comforted the poor Queen, who was under a grievous affliction for having brought into the world such an ugly brat. It is true, that this child no sooner began to prattle, but he said a thousand pretty things, and that in all his actions there was something so taking, that he charmed every-body. I forgot to tell you, that he came into the world with a little tuft of hair upon his head, which made them call him Riquet with the Tuft, for Riquet was the family name.

Seven or eight years after this, the Queen of a neighbouring kingdom was delivered of two daughters at a birth. The first-born of these was beautiful beyond compare, whereat the Queen was so very glad, that those present were afraid that her excess of joy would do her harm. The same Fairy, who had assisted at the birth of little Riquet with the Tuft, was here also; and, to moderate the Queen's gladness, she declared, that this little Princess should have no wit at all,

95

but be as stupid as she was pretty. This mortified the Queen extreamly, but some moments afterwards she had far greater sorrow; for, the second daughter she was delivered of, was very ugly.

"Do not afflict yourself so much, Madam," said the Fairy; "your daughter shall have so great a portion of wit, that her want of beauty will scarcely be perceived."

"God grant it," replied the Queen; "but is there no way to make the eldest, who is so pretty, have some little wit?"

"I can do nothing for her, Madam, as to wit," answered the Fairy, "but everything as to beauty; and as there is nothing but what I would do for your satisfaction, I give her for gift, that she shall have the power to make handsome the person who shall best please her."

As these Princesses grew up, their perfections grew up with them; all the public talk was of the beauty of the eldest, and the wit of the youngest. It is true also that their defects increased considerably with their age; the youngest visibly grew uglier and uglier, and the eldest became every day more and more stupid; she either made no answer at all to what was asked her, or said something very silly; she was with all this so unhandy, that she could not place four pieces of china upon the mantlepiece, without breaking one of them, nor drink a glass of water without spilling half of it upon her cloaths. Tho' beauty is a very great advantage in young people, yet here the youngest sister bore away the bell, almost always, in all companies from the eldest; people would indeed, go first to the Beauty to look upon, and admire her, but turn aside soon after to the Wit, to hear a thousand most entertaining and agreeable turns, and it was amazing to see, in less than a quarter of an hour's time, the eldest with not a soul with her and the whole company crowding about the youngest. The eldest, tho' she was unaccountably dull, could not but notice it, and would have given all her beauty to have half the wit of her sister. The Queen, prudent as she was, could not help reproaching her several times, which had like to have made this poor Princess die for grief.

One day, as she retired into the wood to bewail her misfortune, she saw, coming to her, a little man, very disagreeable, but most magnificently dressed. This was the young Prince Riquet with the Tuft, who having fallen in love with her, by seeing her picture, many of which went all the world over, had left his father's kingdom, to have the pleasure of seeing and talking with her.

Overjoyed to find her thus all alone, he addressed himself to her with all imaginable politeness and respect. Having observed, after he had made her the ordinary compliments, that she was extremely melancholy, he said to her:

" I cannot comprehend, Madam, how a person so beautiful as you are, can be so sorrowful as you seem to be; for tho' I can boast of having seen infinite numbers of ladies exquisitely charming, I can say that I never beheld any one whose beauty approaches yours."

"You are pleased to say so," answered the Princess, and here she stopped.

"Beauty," replied Riquet with the Tuft, "is such a great advantage, that it ought to take the place of all things; and since you possess this treasure, I see nothing that can possibly very much afflict you."

"I had far rather," cried the Princess, "be as ugly as you are, and have wit, than have the beauty I possess, and be so stupid as I am."

"There is nothing, Madam," returned he, "shews more that we have wit, than to believe we have none; and it is the nature of that excellent quality, that the more people have of it, the more they believe they want it."

"I do not know that," said the Princess; "but I know, very well, that I am very senseless, and thence proceeds the vexation which almost kills me."

"If that be all, Madam, which troubles you, I can very easily put an end to your affliction."

"And how will you do that?" cried the Princess.

"I have the power, Madam," replied Riquet with the Tuft, "to give to that person whom I shall love best, as much wit as can be had; and as you, Madam, are that very person, it will be your fault only, if you have not as great a share of it as any one living, provided you will be pleased to marry me."

The Princess remained quite astonished, and answered not a word.

"THE PRINCE BELIEVED HE HAD GIVEN HER MORE WIT THAN HE HAD RESERVED FOR HIMSELF"

"I see," replied Riquet with the Tuft, "that this proposal makes you very uneasy, and I do not wonder at it, but I will give you a whole year to consider of it."

The Princess had so little wit, and, at the same time, so great a longing to have some, that she imagined the end of that year would never be; therefore she accepted the proposal which was made her. She had no sooner promised Riquet with the Tuft that she would marry him on that day twelve-month, than she found herself quite otherwise than she was before; she had an incredible facility of speaking whatever she pleased, after a polite, easy, and natural manner; she began that moment a very gallant conversation with Riquet with the Tuft, wherein she tattled at such a rate, that Riquet with the Tuft believed he had given her more wit than he had reserved for himself.

When she returned to the palace, the whole Court knew not what to think of such a sudden and extraordinary change; for they heard from her now as much sensible discourse, and as many infinitely witty turns, as they had stupid and silly impertinences before. The whole Court was over-joyed at it beyond imagination; it pleased all but her younger sister; because having no longer the advantage of her in respect of wit, she appeared, in comparison of her, a very disagreeable, homely puss. The King governed himself by her advice, and would even sometimes hold a council in her apartment. The noise of this change spreading every where, all the young Princes of the neighbouring kingdoms strove all they could to gain her favour, and almost all of them asked her in marriage; but she found not one of them had wit enough for her, and she gave them all a hearing, but would not engage herself to any.

However, there came one so powerful, rich, witty and handsome, that she could not help having a good inclination for him. Her father perceived it, and told her that she was her own mistress as to the choice of a husband, and that she might declare her intentions. As the more wit we have, the greater difficulty we find to make a firm resolution upon such affairs, this made her desire her father, after having thanked him, to give her time to consider of it.

She went accidentally to walk in the same wood where she met Riquet with the Tuft, to think, the more conveniently, what she ought to do. While she was walking in a profound meditation, she heard a confused noise under her feet, as it were of a great many people who went backwards and forwards, and were very busy. Having listened more attentively, she heard one say:

"Bring me that pot"; another "Give me that kettle"; and a third, "Put some wood upon the fire."

The ground at the same time opened, and she seemingly saw under her feet, a great kitchen full of cooks, scullions, and all sorts of servants necessary for a magnificent entertainment. There came out of it a company of roasters, to the number of twenty, or thirty, who went to plant themselves in a fine alley of wood, about a very long table, with their larding pins in their hands, and skewers in their caps, who began to work, keeping time, to the tune of a very harmonious song.

The Princess, all astonished at this sight, asked them who they worked for.

"For Prince Riquet with the Tuft," said the chief of them, "who is to be married to-morrow."

The Princess was more surprised than ever, and recollecting that it was now that day twelvemonth on which she had promised to marry Riquet with the Tuft, she was like to sink into the ground.

What made her forget this was that, when she made this promise, she was very silly, and having obtained that vast stock of wit which the Prince had bestowed on her, she had intirely forgot her stupidity. She continued walking, but had not taken thirty steps before Riquet with the Tuft presented himself to her, bravely and most magnificently dressed, like a Prince who was going to be married.

"You see, Madam," said he, "I am very exact in keeping my word, and doubt not, in the least, but you are come hither to perform yours, and to make me, by giving me your hand, the happiest of men."

"I shall freely own to you," answered the Princess, "that I have not yet taken any resolution on this affair, and believe I never shall take such a one as you desire."

"You astonish me, Madam," said Riquet with the Tuft.

"I believe it," said the Princess, "and surely if I had to

do with a clown, or a man of no wit, I should find myself
very much at a loss. 'A Princess always observes her word,'
would he say to me, 'and you must marry me, since you
promised to do so.' But as he whom I talk to is the man of
the world who is master of the greatest sense and judgment,
I am sure he will hear reason. You know, that when I was
but a fool, I could, notwithstanding, never come to a resolution
to marry you; why will you have me, now I have so much
judgment as you gave me, and which makes me a more
difficult person than I was at that time, to come to such a
resolution, which I could not then determine to agree to? If
you sincerely thought to make me your wife, you have been
greatly in the wrong to deprive me of my dull simplicity, and
make me see things much more clearly than I did."

"If a man of no wit and sense," replied Riquet with the
Tuft, "would be entitled, as you say, to reproach you for
breach of your word, why will you not let me, Madam, do
likewise in a matter wherein all the happiness of my life is
concerned? Is it reasonable that persons of wit and sense
should be in a worse condition than those who have none?
Can you pretend this; you who have so great a share, and
desired so earnestly to have it? But let us come to fact, if
you please. Setting aside my ugliness and deformity, is there
any thing in me which displeases you? Are you dissatisfied
with my birth, my wit, humour, or manners?"

"Not at all," answered the Princess; "I love you and
respect you in all that you mention." "If it be so," said

"RIQUET WITH THE TUFT APPEARED TO HER THE FINEST PRINCE UPON EARTH"

Riquet with the Tuft, "I am like to be happy, since it is in your power to make me the most lovable of men."

"How can that be?" said the Princess.

"It will come about," said Riquet with the Tuft; "if you love me enough to wish it to be so; and that you may no ways doubt, Madam, of what I say, know that the same Fairy, who, on my birth-day, gave me for gift the power of making the person who should please me extremely witty and judicious, has, in like manner, given you for gift the power of making him, whom you love, and would grant that favour to, extremely handsome."

"If it be so," said the Princess, "I wish, with all my heart, that you may be the most lovable Prince in the world, and I bestow it on you, as much as I am able."

The Princess had no sooner pronounced these words, but Riquet with the Tuft appeared to her the finest Prince upon earth; the handsomest and most amiable man she ever saw. Some affirm that it was not the enchantments of the Fairy which worked this change, but that love alone caused the metamorphosis. They say, that the Princess, having made due reflection on the perseverance of her lover, his discretion, and all the good qualities of his mind, his wit and judgment, saw no longer the deformity of his body, nor the ugliness of his face; that his hump seemed to her no more than the homely air of one who has a broad back; and that whereas till then she saw him limp horribly, she found it nothing more than a certain sidling air, which charmed her.

They say farther, that his eyes, which were very squinting, seemed to her all the more bright and sparkling ; that their irregularity passed in her judgment for a mark of a violent excess of love ; and, in short, that his great red nose had, in her opinion, somewhat of the martial and heroic.

Howsoever it was, the Princess promised immediately to marry him, on condition he obtained her father's consent. The King being acquainted that his daughter had abundance of esteem for Riquet with the Tuft, whom he knew otherwise for a most sage and judicious Prince, received him for his son-in-law with pleasure ; and the next morning their nuptials were celebrated, as Riquet with the Tuft had foreseen, and according to the orders he had a long time before given.

The Moral

What in this little Tale we find,
Is less a fable than real truth.
In those we love appear rare gifts of mind,
And body too : wit, judgment, beauty, youth.

Another

A countenance whereon, by nature's hand,
Beauty is trac'd, also the lively stain
Of such complexion art can ne'er attain,
With all these gifts hath not so much command
On hearts, as hath one secret charm alone.
Love finds that out, to all besides unknown.

Little Thumb

"LITTLE THUMB WAS AS GOOD AS HIS WORD, AND RETURNED THAT SAME NIGHT WITH THE NEWS"

(page 123)

▫ Little ▫ Thumb ▫

THERE was, once upon a time, a man and his wife, faggot-makers by trade, who had seven children, all boys. The eldest was but ten years old, and the youngest only seven. One might wonder how that the faggot-maker could have so many children in so little a time; but it was because his wife went nimbly about her business and never brought fewer than two at a birth. They were very poor, and their seven children incommoded them greatly, because not one of them was able to earn his bread. That which gave them yet more uneasiness was, that the youngest was of a very puny constitution, and scarce ever spake a word, which made them take that for stupidity which was a sign of good sense. He was very little, and, when born, no bigger than one's thumb; which made him be called Little Thumb.

The poor child bore the blame of whatsoever was done amiss in the house, and guilty or not was always in the wrong; he was, notwithstanding, more cunning and had a far greater share of wisdom than all his brothers put together, and if he spake little he heard and thought the more.

There happened now to come a very bad year, and the famine was so great, that these poor people resolved to rid themselves of their children. One evening, when they were all in bed and the faggot-maker was sitting with his wife at the fire, he said to her, with his heart ready to burst with grief:

"Thou see'st plainly that we are not able to keep our children, and I cannot see them starve to death before my face; I am resolved to lose them in the wood to-morrow, which may very easily be done; for while they are busy in tying up the faggots, we may run away, and leave them, without their taking any notice."

"Ah!" cried out his wife, "and can'st thou thyself have the heart to take thy children out along with thee on purpose to lose them?"

In vain did her husband represent to her their extreme poverty; she would not consent to it; she was, indeed poor, but she was their mother. However, having considered what a grief it would be to her to see them perish with hunger, she at last consented and went to bed all in tears.

Little Thumb heard every word that had been spoken; for observing, as he lay in his bed, that they were talking very busily, he had got up softly and hid himself under his father's stool, that he might hear what they said, without being seen. He went to bed again, but did not sleep a wink all the rest of the night, thinking on what he ought to do. He got up early in the morning, and went to the river side, where he filled his pockets full of small white pebbles, and then returned home. They all went abroad, but Little Thumb never told his brothers one syllable of what he knew. They went into a very thick forest, where they could not see one another at ten paces distance. The faggot-maker began to cut wood, and the children to gather up sticks to make

"HE BROUGHT THEM HOME BY THE VERY SAME WAY THEY CAME"

faggots. Their father and mother seeing them busy at their work, got from them by degrees, and then ran away from them all at once, along a by-way, thro' the winding bushes.

When the children saw they were left alone, they began to cry as loud as they could. Little Thumb let them cry on, knowing very well how to go home again; for as he came he had taken care to drop all along the way the little white pebbles he had in his pockets. Then said he to them:

" Be not afraid, brothers, father and mother have left us here, but I will lead you home again, only follow me." They did so, and he brought them home by the very same way they came into the forest. They dared not to go in, but sat themselves down at the door, listening to what their father and mother were saying.

The very moment the faggot-maker and his wife were got home, the lord of the manor sent them ten crowns, which he had owed them a long while, and which they never expected. This gave them new life; for the poor people were almost famished. The faggot-maker sent his wife immediately to the butcher's. As it was a long while since they had eaten a bit, she bought thrice as much meat as would sup two people. Having filled their bellies, the woman said:

" Alas! where are now our poor children? They would make a good feast of what we have left here; but then it was you, William, who had a mind to lose them; I told you we should repent of it: what are they now doing in the forest? Alas! dear God, the wolves have, perhaps, already eaten them up: thou art very inhuman thus to have lost thy children."

The faggot-maker grew at last quite out of patience, for she repeated this above twenty times, that they should repent of it, and she was in the right of it for so saying. He threatened to beat her, if she did not hold her tongue. It was not that the faggot-maker was not, perhaps, more vexed than his wife, but that she teized him, and that he was of the humour of a great many others, who love wives who speak right, but think those very importunate who are always in the right. She was half drowned in tears, crying out:

"Alas! where are now my children, my poor children?"

She spake this so very loud, that the children who were at the door, began to cry out all together:

"Here we are, here we are."

She ran immediately to open the door, and said, hugging them:

"I am glad to see you, my dear children; you are very hungry and weary; and my poor Peter, thou art horribly bemired; come in and let me clean thee."

Now, you must know, that Peter was her eldest son, whom she loved above all the rest, because he was somewhat carrotty, as she herself was. They sat down to supper, and ate with such a good appetite as pleased both father and mother, whom they acquainted how frightened they were in the forest; speaking almost always all together. The good folks were extremely glad to see their children once more at home, and this joy continued while the ten crowns lasted; but when the money was all gone, they fell again into their former uneasiness, and resolved to lose them again; and, that they might be the surer of doing it, to carry them at a much greater distance than before. They could not talk of this so secretly, but they were overheard by Little Thumb, who made account to get out of this difficulty as well as the former; but though he got up betimes in the morning, to go and pick up some little pebbles, he was disappointed; for he found the housedoor double-locked, and was at a stand what to do. When their father had given each of them a piece of bread for their breakfast, he fancied he might make use of this bread instead of the pebbles, by throwing it in little bits all along the way they should pass; and so he put it up into his pocket.

Their father and mother brought them into the thickest and most obscure part of the forest; when, stealing away into a by-path, they there left them. Little Thumb was not very uneasy at it; for he thought he could easily find the way again, by means of his bread which he had scattered all along as he came. But he was very much surprised when he could not find so much as one crumb; the birds had come and eaten it up every bit. They were now in great affliction, for the farther they went, the more they were out of their way, and were more and more bewildered in the forest.

Night now came on, and there arose a terrible high wind, which made them dreadfully afraid. They fancied they heard on every side of them the houling of wolves coming to eat them up; they scarce dared to speak, or turn their heads. After this, it rained very hard, which wet them to the skin; their feet slipped at every step they took, and they fell into the mire, whence they got up in a very dirty pickle; their hands were in a sorry state.

Little Thumb climbed up to the top of a tree, to see if he could discover any thing; and having turned his head about on every side, he saw at last a glimmering light, like that of a candle, but a long way from the forest. He came down, and, when upon the ground, he could see it no more, which grieved him sadly. However, having walked for some time with his brothers towards that side on which he had seen the light, he perceived it again as he came out of the wood.

They came at last to the house where this candle was, not without abundance of fear; for very often they lost sight of it, which happened every time they came into a bottom. They knocked at the door, and a good woman came and open'd it; she asked them what they wished.

Little Thumb told her they were poor children who had been lost in the forest, and desired to lodge there for God's sake. The woman seeing them so very pretty, began to weep, and said to them:

"Alas! poor babies, whither are ye come? Do ye know that this house belongs to a cruel Ogre, who eats up little children?"

"Ah! dear Madam," answered Little Thumb (who

trembled every joint of him, as well as his brothers) "what shall we do? To be sure, the wolves of the forest will devour us to-night, if you refuse us to lie here; and so, we would rather the gentleman should eat us. Perhaps he will take pity on us, especially if you please to beg it of him."

The Ogre's wife, who believed she could conceal them from her husband till morning, let them come in, and brought them to warm themselves at a very good fire; for there was a whole sheep upon the spit roasting for the Ogre's supper.

As they began to be a little warm, they heard three or four great raps at the door; this was the Ogre, who was come home. Upon this she hid them under the bed, and went to open the door. The Ogre presently asked if supper was ready, and the wine drawn; and then he sat himself down to table. The sheep was as yet all raw and bloody; but he liked it the better for that. He sniffed about to the right and left, saying, "I smell fresh meat."

"What you smell so," said his wife, "must be the calf which I have just now killed and flayed."

"I smell fresh meat, I tell thee once more," replied the Ogre, looking crossly at his wife, "and there is something here which I do not understand."

As he spake these words, he got up from the table, and went directly to the bed.

"Ah!" said he, "I see how thou would'st cheat me, thou cursed woman; I know not why I do not eat up thee too; but it is well for thee that thou art a tough old carrion.

117

Here is good game, which comes very luckily to entertain three Ogres of my acquaintance, who are to pay me a visit in a day or two."

With that he dragged them out from under the bed one by one. The poor children fell upon their knees, and begged his pardon; but they had to do with one of the most cruel Ogres in the world, who, far from having any pity on them, had already devoured them with his eyes; he told his wife they would be delicate eating, when tossed up with good savoury sauce. He then took a great knife, and coming up to these poor children, whetted it upon a great whet-stone which he held in his left hand. He had already taken hold of one of them, when his wife said to him:

"What need you do it now? It is time enough to-morrow?"

"Hold your prattling," said the Ogre, "they will eat the tenderer."

"But you have so much meat already," replied his wife, "you have no occasion. Here is a calf, two sheep, and half a hog."

"That is true," said the Ogre, "give them their belly-full, that they may not fall away, and put them to bed."

The good woman was overjoyed at this, and gave them a good supper; but they were so much afraid, they could not eat a bit. As for the Ogre, he sat down again to drink, being highly pleased that he had got wherewithal to treat his friends. He drank a dozen glasses more than ordinary, which got up into his head, and obliged him to go to bed.

The Ogre had seven daughters, all little children, and these young Ogresses had all of them very fine complexions, because they used to eat fresh meat like their father; but they had little grey eyes, quite round, hooked noses, wide mouths, and very long sharp teeth standing at a good distance from each other. They were not as yet over and above mischievous; but they promised very fair for it, for they already bit little children, that they might suck their blood. They had been put to bed early, with every one a crown of gold upon her head. There was in the same chamber another bed of the like bigness, and it was into this bed the Ogre's wife put the seven little boys; after which she went to bed to her husband.

Little Thumb, who had observed that the Ogre's daughters had crowns of gold upon their heads, and was afraid lest the Ogre should repent his not killing them, got up about midnight; and taking his brothers' bonnets and his own, went very softly, put them upon the heads of the seven little Ogresses, after having taken off their crowns of gold, which he put upon his own head and his brothers', that the Ogre might take them for his daughters, and his daughters for the little boys whom he wanted to kill. All this succeeded according to his desire; for the Ogre waking about midnight, and sorry that he deferred to do that till morning which he might have done over-night, threw himself hastily out of bed, and taking his great knife:

" Let us see," said he, " how our little rogues do, and not make two jobs of the matter."

He then went up, groping all the way, into his daughters' chamber; and came to the bed where the little boys lay, who were every soul of them fast asleep; except Little Thumb, who was terribly afraid when he found the Ogre fumbling about his head, as he had done about his brothers'. The Ogre, feeling the golden crowns, said:

" I should have made a fine piece of work of it truly; I find I guzzled too much last night."

Then he went to the bed where the girls lay; and having found the boys' little bonnets: " Hah!" said he, " my merry lads, are you there? Let us to work!"

And saying these words, without more ado, he cut the throats of all his seven daughters.

Well pleased with what he had done, he went to bed again to his wife. So soon as Little Thumb heard the Ogre snore, he waked his brothers, and bade them put on their clothes presently, and follow him. They stole down softly into the garden, and got over the wall. They kept running almost all night, trembling all the while, without knowing which way they went.

The Ogre, when he waked, said to his wife:

" Go up stairs and dress those young rascals who came here last night."

The Ogress was very much surprised at this goodness of her husband, not dreaming after what manner he intended she should dress them; but thinking that he had ordered her to go and put on their cloaths, went up, and was strangely astonished when she perceived her seven daughters killed, and weltering in their blood. She fainted away; for this is the first expedient almost all women find in such-like cases. The Ogre, fearing his wife would be too long in doing what he had ordered, went up himself to help her. He was no less amazed than his wife, at this frightful spectacle.

"Ah! what have I done?" cried he. "The cursed wretches shall pay for it, and that instantly."

He threw then a pitcher of water upon his wife's face; and having brought her to herself:

"Give me quickly," cried he, "my boots of seven leagues, that I may go and catch them."

He went out; and, having run over a vast deal of ground, both on this side and that, he came at last into the very road where the poor children were, and not above a hundred paces from their father's house. They espied the Ogre, who went at one step from mountain to mountain, and over rivers as easily as the narrowest kennels.[1] Little Thumb, seeing a hollow rock near the place where they were, made his brothers hide themselves in it, and crowded into it himself, minding always what would become of the Ogre.

The Ogre, who found himself much tired with his long and fruitless journey (for these boots of seven leagues extremely fatigue the wearer), had a great mind to rest him-

[1] That is, 'channels.'

self, and, by chance, went to sit down upon the rock where these little boys had hid themselves. As he was worn out, he fell asleep : and, after reposing himself some time he began to snore so frightfully, that the poor children were no less afraid of him, than when he held up his great knife, and was going to cut their throats. Little Thumb was not so much frightened as his brothers, and told them that they should run away immediately towards home, while the Ogre was asleep so soundly ; and that they should not be anxious about him. They took his advice, and got home presently. Little Thumb came up to the Ogre, pulled off his boots gently, and put them on upon his own legs. The boots were very long and large ; but as they were Fairies, they had the gift of becoming big and little, according to the legs of those who wore them ; so that they fitted his feet and legs as well as if they had been made on purpose for him.

He went immediately to the Ogre's house, where he saw his wife crying bitterly for the loss of her murdered daughters.

"Your husband," said Little Thumb, " is in very great danger, being taken by a gang of thieves, who have sworn to kill him, if he does not give them all his gold and silver. Just when they held their daggers at his throat, he perceived me, and desired me to come and tell you the condition he is in, and that you should give me whatsoever he has of value, without retaining any one thing ; for otherwise they will kill him without mercy ; and, as his case is very pressing, he desired me to make use (you see I have them on) of his boots, that I might make the more haste, and to shew you that I do not impose upon you."

The good woman, being sadly frightened, gave him all she had : for this Ogre was a very good husband, tho' he used to eat up little children. Little Thumb, having thus got all the Ogre's money, came home to his father's house, where he was received with abundance of joy.

There are many people who do not agree in this circumstance, and pretend that Little Thumb never robbed the Ogre at all, and that he only thought he might very justly, and with safe conscience take off his boots of seven leagues, because he made no other use of them, but to run after little children. These folks affirm, that they were very well assured of this, and the more, as having drank and eaten often at the faggot-maker's house. They aver, that, when Little Thumb had taken off the Ogre's boots, he went to Court, where he was informed that they were very anxious about a certain army, which was two hundred leagues off, and the success of a battle. He went, say they, to the King, and told him that, if he desired it, he would bring him news from the army before night. The King promised him a great sum of money upon that condition. Little Thumb was as good as his word, and returned that very same night with the news ; and this first expedition causing him to be known, he got whatever he pleased ; for the King paid him very well for carrying his orders to the army, and abundance of ladies gave him what he would to bring them news from their lovers ; and that this was his greatest gain. There were some married women, too, who sent letters by him to their husbands, but they paid him so ill that it was not worth his while, and turned to such small account, that he scorned ever to reckon what he got that way. After having, for some time, carried on the business of a messenger, and gained thereby great wealth, he went home to his father, where it was impossible to express the joy they were all in at his return. He made the whole family very well-to-do, bought places for his father and brothers ; and by that means settled them very handsomely in the world, and, in the mean time, rose high in the King's favour.

The Moral

At many children parents don't repine,
If they are handsome; in their judgment shine;
Polite in carriage are, in body strong,
Graceful in mien, and elegant in tongue.
But if perchance an offspring prove but weak,
Him they revile, laugh at, defraud and cheat.
Such is the wretched world's curs'd way; and yet
Sometimes this urchin whom despis'd we see,
Through unforeseen events doth honour get,
And fortune bring to all his family.

The ▫ Ridiculous ▫ Wishes

IN days long past there lived a poor woodcutter who found life very hard. Indeed, it was his lot to toil for little guerdon, and although he was young and happily married there were moments when he wished himself dead and below ground.

One day while at his work he was again lamenting his fate.

"Some men," he said, "have only to make known their desires, and straightway these are granted, and their every wish fulfilled; but it has availed me little to wish for ought, for the gods are deaf to the prayers of such as I."

As he spoke these words there was a great noise of thunder, and Jupiter appeared before him wielding his mighty thunderbolts. Our poor man was stricken with fear and threw himself on the ground.

"My lord," he said, "forget my foolish speech; heed not my wishes, but cease thy thundering!"

"Have no fear," answered Jupiter; "I have heard thy plaint, and have come hither to show thee how greatly thou dost wrong me. Hark! I, who am sovereign lord of this world, promise to grant in full the first three wishes which it will please thee to utter, whatever these may be. Consider well what things can bring thee joy and prosperity, and as thy happiness is at stake, be not over-hasty, but revolve the matter in thy mind."

Having thus spoken Jupiter withdrew himself and made

his ascent to Olympus. As for our woodcutter, he blithely corded his faggot, and throwing it over his shoulder, made for his home. To one so light of heart the load also seemed light, and his thoughts were merry as he strode along. Many a wish came into his mind, but he was resolved to seek the advice of his wife, who was a young woman of good understanding.

He had soon reached his cottage, and casting down his faggot:

"Behold me, Fanny," he said. "Make up the fire and spread the board, and let there be no stint. We are wealthy, Fanny, wealthy for evermore; we have only to wish for whatsoever we may desire."

Thereupon he told her the story of what had befallen that day. Fanny, whose mind was quick and active, immediately conceived many plans for the advancement of their fortune, but she approved her husband's resolve to act with prudence and circumspection.

"'Twere a pity," she said, " to spoil our chances through impatience. We had best take counsel of the night, and wish no wishes until to-morrow."

"That is well spoken," answered Harry. "Meanwhile fetch a bottle of our best, and we shall drink to our good fortune."

Fanny brought a bottle from the store behind the faggots, and our man enjoyed his ease, leaning back in his chair with his toes to the fire and his goblet in his hand.

"A LONG BLACK PUDDING CAME WINDING AND WRIGGLING TOWARDS HER"

"What fine glowing embers!" he said, "and what a fine toasting fire! I wish we had a black pudding at hand."

Hardly had he spoken these words when his wife beheld, to her great astonishment, a long black pudding which, issuing from a corner of the hearth, came winding and wriggling towards her. She uttered a cry of fear, and then again exclaimed in dismay, when she perceived that this strange occurrence was due to the wish which her husband had so rashly and foolishly spoken. Turning upon him, in her anger and disappointment she called the poor man all the abusive names that she could think of.

"What!" she said to him, "when you can call for a kingdom, for gold, pearls, rubies, diamonds, for princely garments and wealth untold, is this the time to set your mind upon black puddings!"

"Nay!" answered the man, "'twas a thoughtless speech, and a sad mistake; but I shall now be on my guard, and shall do better next time."

"Who knows that you will?" returned his wife. "Once a witless fool, always a witless fool!" and giving free rein to her vexation and ill-temper she continued to upbraid her husband until his anger also was stirred, and he had wellnigh made a second bid and wished himself a widower.

"Enough! woman," he cried at last; "put a check upon thy froward tongue! Who ever heard such impertinence as this! A plague on the shrew and on her pudding! Would to heaven it hung at the end of her nose!"

No sooner had the husband given voice to these words than the wish was straightway granted, and the long coil of black pudding appeared grafted to the angry dame's nose.

Our man paused when he beheld what he had wrought. Fanny was a comely young woman, and blest with good looks, and truth to tell, this new ornament did not set off her beauty. Yet it offered one advantage, that as it hung right before her mouth, it would thus effectively curb her speech.

So, having now but one wish left, he had all but resolved to make good use of it without further delay, and, before any other mischance could befall, to wish himself a kingdom of his own. He was about to speak the word, when he was stayed by a sudden thought.

"It is true," he said to himself, "that there is none so great as a King, but what of the Queen that must share his dignity? With what grace would she sit beside me on the throne with a yard of black pudding for a nose?"

In this dilemma he resolved to put the case to Fanny, and to leave her to decide whether she would rather be a Queen, with this most horrible appendage marring her good looks, or remain a peasant wife, but with her shapely nose relieved of this untoward addition.

Fanny's mind was soon made up: although she had

"TRUTH TO TELL, THIS NEW ORNAMENT DID NOT SET OFF HER BEAUTY"

dreamt of a crown and sceptre, yet a woman's first wish is always to please. To this great desire all else must yield, and Fanny would rather be fair in drugget than be a Queen with an ugly face.

Thus our woodcutter did not change his state, did not become a potentate, nor fill his purse with golden crowns. He was thankful enough to use his remaining wish to a more humble purpose, and forthwith relieved his wife of her encumbrance.

The Moral

Ah ! so it is that miserable man,
By nature fickle, blind, unwise, and rash,
Oft fails to reap a harvest from great gifts
Bestowed upon him by the heav'nly gods.

Donkey-skin

"ANOTHER GOWN THE COLOUR OF THE MOON"

(page 145)

▫ Donkey-skin ▫

ONCE upon a time there was a King, so great, so beloved by his people, and so respected by all his neighbours and allies that one might almost say he was the happiest monarch alive. His good fortune was made even greater by the choice he had made for wife of a Princess as beautiful as she was virtuous, with whom he lived in perfect happiness. Now, of this chaste marriage was born a daughter endowed with so many gifts that they had no regret because other children were not given to them.

Magnificence, good taste, and abundance reigned in the palace; there were wise and clever ministers, virtuous and devoted courtiers, faithful and diligent servants. The spacious stables were filled with the most beautiful horses in the world, and coverts of rich caparison; but what most astonished strangers who came to admire them was to see, in the finest stall, a master donkey, with great long ears.

Now, it was not for a whim but for a good reason that the King had given this donkey a particular and distinguished place. The special qualities of this rare animal deserved the distinction, since nature had made it in so extraordinary a way that its litter, instead of being like that of other donkeys, was covered every morning with an abundance of beautiful golden crowns, and golden louis of every kind, which were collected daily.

Since the vicissitudes of life wait on Kings as much as on their subjects, and good is always mingled with ill, it so befell that the Queen was suddenly attacked by a fatal illness, and, in spite of science, and the skill of the doctors, no remedy could be found. There was great mourning throughout the land. The King who, notwithstanding the famous proverb, that marriage is the tomb of love, was deeply attached to his wife, was distressed beyond measure and made fervent vows to all the temples in his kingdom, and offered to give his life for that of his beloved consort; but he invoked the gods and the Fairies in vain. The Queen, feeling her last hour approach, said to her husband, who was dissolved in tears: "It is well that I should speak to you of a certain matter before I die: if, perchance, you should desire to marry again . . ." At these words the King broke into piteous cries, took his wife's hands in his own, and assured her that it was useless to speak to him of a second marriage.

"No, my dear spouse," he said at last, "speak to me rather of how I may follow you."

"The State," continued the Queen with a finality which but increased the laments of the King, "the State demands successors, and since I have only given you a daughter, it will urge you to beget sons who resemble you; but I ask you earnestly not to give way to the persuasions of your people until you have found a Princess more beautiful and more perfectly fashioned than I. I beg you to swear this to me, and then I shall die content."

Perchance, the Queen, who did not lack self-esteem, exacted this oath firmly believing that there was not her equal in the world, and so felt assured that the King would never marry again. Be this as it may, at length she died, and never did husband make so much lamentation; the King wept and sobbed day and night, and the punctilious fulfilment of the rites of widower-hood, even the smallest, was his sole occupation.

But even great griefs do not last for ever. After a time the magnates of the State assembled and came to the King, urging him to take another wife. At first this request seemed hard to him and made him shed fresh tears. He pleaded the vows he had made to the Queen, and defied his counsellors to find a Princess more beautiful and better fashioned than was she, thinking this to be impossible. But the Council treated the promise as a trifle, and said that it mattered little about beauty if the Queen were but virtuous and fruitful. For the State needed Princes for its peace and prosperity, and though, in truth, the Princess, his daughter, had all the qualities requisite for making a great Queen, yet of necessity she must choose an alien for her husband, and then the stranger would take her away with him. If, on the other hand, he remained in her country and shared the throne with her, their children would not be considered to be of pure native stock, and so, there being no Prince of his name, neighbouring peoples would stir up wars, and the kingdom would be ruined.

The King, impressed by these considerations, promised that he would think over the matter. And so search was made among all the marriageable Princesses for one that would suit him. Every day charming portraits were brought him, but none gave promise of the beauty of his late Queen; instead of coming to a decision he brooded over his sorrow until in the end his reason left him. In his delusions he imagined himself once more a young man; he thought the Princess his daughter, in her youth and beauty, was his Queen as he had known her in the days of their courtship, and living thus in the past he urged the unhappy girl to speedily become his bride.

The young Princess, who was virtuous and chaste, threw herself at the feet of the King her father and conjured him, with all the eloquence she could command, not to constrain her to consent to his unnatural desire.

The King, in his madness, could not understand the reason of her desperate reluctance, and asked an old Druid-priest to set the conscience of the Princess at rest. Now this Druid, less religious than ambitious, sacrificed the cause of innocence and virtue to the favour of so great a monarch, and instead of trying to restore the King to his right mind, he encouraged him in his delusion.

The young Princess, beside herself with misery, at last bethought her of the Lilac-fairy, her godmother; determined to consult her, she set out that same night in a pretty little carriage drawn by a great sheep who knew all the roads. When she arrived the Fairy, who loved the Princess, told her that she knew all she had come to say, but that she need have

"HE THOUGHT THE PRINCESS WAS HIS QUEEN"

no fear, for nothing would harm her if only she faithfully fulfilled the Fairy's injunctions. "For, my dear child," she said to her, "it would be a great sin to submit to your father's wishes, but you can avoid the necessity without displeasing him. Tell him that to satisfy a whim you have, he must give you a dress the colour of the weather. Never, in spite of all his love and his power will he be able to give you that."

The Princess thanked her godmother from her heart, and the next morning spoke to the King as the Fairy had counselled her, and protested that no one would win her hand unless he gave her a dress the colour of the weather. The King, overjoyed and hopeful, called together the most skilful workmen, and demanded this robe of them; otherwise they should be hanged. But he was saved from resorting to this extreme measure, since, on the second day, they brought the much desired robe. The heavens are not a more beautiful blue, when they are girdled with clouds of gold, than was that lovely dress when it was unfolded. The Princess was very sad because of it, and did not know what to do.

Once more she went to her Fairy-godmother who, astonished that her plan had been foiled, now told her to ask for another gown the colour of the moon.

The King again sought out the most clever workmen and expressly commanded them to make a dress the colour of the moon; and woe betide them if between the giving of the order and the bringing of the dress more than twenty-four hours should elapse.

The Princess, though pleased with the dress when it was delivered, gave way to distress when she was with her women and her nurse. The Lilac-fairy, who knew all, hastened to comfort her and said: "Either I am greatly deceived or it is certain that if you ask for a dress the colour of the sun we shall at last baffle the King your father, for it would never be possible to make such a gown; in any case we should gain time."

So the Princess asked for yet another gown as the Fairy bade her. The infatuated King could refuse his daughter nothing, and he gave without regret all the diamonds and rubies in his crown to aid this superb work; nothing was to be spared that could make the dress as beautiful as the sun. And, indeed, when the dress appeared, all those who unfolded it were obliged to close their eyes, so much were they dazzled. And, truth to tell, green spectacles and smoked glasses date from that time.

What was the Princess to do? Never had so beautiful and so artistic a robe been seen. She was dumb-founded, and pretending that its brilliance had hurt her eyes she retired to her chamber, where she found the Fairy awaiting her.

On seeing the dress like the sun, the Lilac-fairy became red with rage. "Oh! this time, my child," she said to the Princess, "we will put the King to terrible proof. In spite of his madness I think he will be a little astonished by the request that I counsel you to make of him; it is that he should give you the skin of that ass he loves so dearly, and which supplies him so profusely with the means of paying all his expenses. Go, and do not fail to tell him that you want this skin. The Princess, overjoyed at finding yet another avenue of escape; for she thought that her father could never bring himself to sacrifice the ass, went to find him, and unfolded to him her latest desire.

Although the King was astonished by this whim, he did not hesitate to satisfy it; the poor ass was sacrificed and the skin brought, with due ceremony, to the Princess, who, seeing no other way of avoiding her ill-fortune, was desperate.

At that moment her godmother arrived. "What are you doing, my child?" she asked, seeing the Princess tearing her hair, her beautiful cheeks stained with tears. "This is the most happy moment of your life. Wrap yourself in this skin, leave the palace, and walk so long as you can find ground to carry you: when one sacrifices everything to virtue the gods know how to mete out reward. Go, and I will take care that your possessions follow you; in whatever place you rest, your chest with your clothes and your jewels will follow your steps, and here is my wand which I will give you: tap the ground with it when you have need of the chest, and it will appear before your eyes: but haste to set forth, and do not delay." The Princess embraced her godmother many times, and begged her not to forsake her. Then after she had smeared herself with soot from the chimney, she wrapped herself up in that ugly skin and went out from the magnificent palace without being recognised by a single person.

The absence of the Princess caused a great commotion. The King, who had caused a sumptuous banquet to be prepared, was inconsolable. He sent out more than a hundred gendarmes, and more than a thousand musketeers in quest of her; but the Lilac-fairy made her invisible to the cleverest seekers, and thus she escaped their vigilance.

Meanwhile the Princess walked far, far and even farther away; after a time she sought for a resting place, but although out of charity people gave her food, she was so dishevelled and dirty that no one wanted to keep her. At length she came to a beautiful town, at the gate of which was a small farm. Now the farmer's wife had need of a wench to wash the dishes and to attend to the geese and the pigs, and seeing so dirty a vagrant offered to engage her. The Princess, who was now much fatigued, accepted joyfully. She was put into a recess in the kitchen where for the first days she was subjected to the coarse jokes of the men-servants, so dirty and unpleasant did the donkey-skin make her appear. At last they tired of their pleasantries; moreover she was so attentive to her work that the farmer's wife took her under her protection. She minded the sheep, and penned them up when it was necessary, and she took the geese out to feed with such intelligence that it seemed as if she had never done anything else. Everything that her beautiful hands undertook was done well.

One day she was sitting near a clear fountain where she often repaired to bemoan her sad condition, when she thought she would look at herself in the water. The horrible donkey-skin which covered her from head to toe revolted her. Ashamed, she washed her face and her hands, which became whiter than ivory, and once again her lovely complexion took its natural freshness. The joy of finding herself so beautiful filled her with the desire to bathe in the pool, and this she did. But she had to don her unworthy skin again before she returned to the farm.

By good fortune the next day chanced to be a holiday, and so she had leisure to tap for her chest with the fairy's wand, arrange her toilet, powder her beautiful hair and put on the lovely gown which was the colour of the weather; but the room was so small that the train could not be properly spread out. The beautiful Princess looked at herself, and with good reason, admired her appearance so much that she resolved to wear her magnificent dresses in turn on holidays and Sundays for her own amusement, and this she regularly did. She entwined flowers and diamonds in her lovely hair with admirable art, and often she sighed that she had no witness of her beauty save the sheep and geese, who loved her just as much in the horrible donkey-skin after which she had been named at the farm.

One holiday when Donkey-skin had put on her sun-hued dress, the son of the King to whom the farm belonged alighted there to rest on his return from the hunt. This

Prince was young and handsome, beloved of his father and of the Queen his mother, and adored by the people. After he had partaken of the simple collation which was offered him he set out to inspect the farm-yard and all its nooks and corners. In going thus from place to place, he entered a dark alley at the bottom of which was a closed door. Curiosity made him put his eye to the keyhole. Imagine his astonishment at seeing a Princess so beautiful and so richly dressed, and withal of so noble and dignified a mien, that he took her to be a divinity. The impetuosity of his feelings at this moment would have made him force the door, had it not been for the respect with which that charming figure filled him.

It was with difficulty that he withdrew from this gloomy little alley, intent on discovering who the inmate of the tiny room might be. He was told that it was a scullion called Donkey-skin because of the skin which she always wore, and that she was so dirty and unpleasant that no one took any notice of her, or even spoke to her; she had just been taken out of pity to look after the geese.

The Prince, though little satisfied by this information, saw that these dense people knew no more, and that it was useless to question them. So he returned to the palace of the King his father, beyond words in love, having continually before his eyes the beautiful image of the goddess whom he had seen through the keyhole. He was full of regret that he had not knocked at the door, and promised

"CURIOSITY MADE HIM PUT HIS EYE TO THE KEYHOLE"

himself that he would not fail to do so next time. But the fervency of his love caused him such great agitation that the same night he was seized by a terrible fever, and was soon at death's door. The Queen, who had no other child, was in despair because all remedies proved useless. In vain she promised great rewards to the doctors; though they exerted all their skill, nothing would cure the Prince. At last they decided that some great sorrow had caused this terrible fever. They told the Queen, who, full of tenderness for her son, went to him and begged him to tell her his trouble. She declared that even if it was a matter of giving him the crown, his father would yield the throne to him without regret; or if he desired some Princess, even though there should be war with the King her father and their subjects should, with reason, complain, all should be sacrificed to obtain what he wished. She implored him with tears not to die, since their life depended on his. The Queen did not finish this touching discourse without moving the Prince to tears.

"Madam," he said at last, in a very feeble voice, "I am not so base that I desire the crown of my father, rather may Heaven grant him life for many years, and that I may always be the most faithful and the most respectful of his subjects! As to the Princesses that you speak of, I have never yet thought of marriage, and you well know that, subject as I am to your wishes, I shall obey, you always, even though it be painful to me."

"Ah! my son," replied the Queen, "we will spare nothing to save your life. But, my dear child, save mine and that of the King your father by telling me what you desire, and be assured that you shall have it."

"Well, Madam," he said, "since you would have me tell you my thought, I obey you. It would indeed be a sin to place in danger two lives so dear to me. Know, my mother, that I wish Donkey-skin to make me a cake, and to have it brought to me when it is ready."

The Queen, astonished at this strange name, asked who Donkey-skin might be.

"It is, Madam," replied one of her officers who had by chance seen this girl, "It is the most ugly creature imaginable after the wolf, a slut who lodges at your farm, and minds your geese."

"It matters not," said the Queen; "my son, on his way home from the chase, has perchance eaten of her cakes; it is a whim such as those who are sick do sometimes have. In a word, I wish that Donkey-skin, since Donkey-skin it is, make him presently a cake."

A messenger ran to the farm and told Donkey-skin that she was to make a cake for the Prince as well as she possibly could. Now, some believe that Donkey-skin had been aware of the Prince in her heart at the moment when he had put his eye to the keyhole; and then, looking from her little window, she had seen him, so young, so handsome, and so shapely, that the remembrance of him had remained, and that often the thought of him had cost her some sighs. Be that as it may, Donkey-skin, either having seen him, or having heard him spoken of with praise, was overjoyed to think that she might become known to him. She shut herself in her little room, threw off the ugly skin, bathed her face and hands, arranged her hair, put on a beautiful corsage of bright silver, and an equally beautiful petticoat, and then set herself to make the much desired cake. She took the finest flour, and newest eggs and freshest butter, and while she was working them, whether by design or no, a ring which she had on her finger fell into the cake and was mixed in it. When the cooking was done she muffled herself in her horrible skin and gave the cake to the messenger, asking him for news of the Prince; but the man would not deign to reply, and without a word ran quickly back to the palace.

The Prince took the cake greedily from the man's hands, and ate it with such voracity that the doctors who were present did not fail to say that this haste was not a good sign. Indeed, the Prince came near to being choked by the ring, which he nearly swallowed, in one of the pieces of cake. But he drew it cleverly from his mouth, and his desire for the cake was forgotten as he examined the fine emerald set in a gold keeper-ring, a ring so small that he knew it could only be worn on the prettiest little finger in the world.

He kissed the ring a thousand times, put it under his pillow, and drew it out every moment that he thought himself unobserved. The torment that he gave himself, planning how he might see her to whom the ring belonged, not daring to believe that if he asked for Donkey-skin she would be allowed to come, and not daring to speak of what he had seen through the key-hole for fear that he would be laughed at for a dreamer, brought back the fever with great violence. The doctors, not knowing what more to do, declared to the Queen that the Prince's malady was love, whereupon the Queen and the disconsolate King ran to their son.

"My son, my dear son," cried the affected monarch, "tell us the name of her whom you desire : we swear that we will give her to you. Even though she were the vilest of slaves."

The Queen embracing him, agreed with all that the King had said, and the Prince, moved by their tears and caresses, said to them : "My father and my mother, I in no way desire to make a marriage which is displeasing to you." And drawing the emerald from under his pillow he added : "To prove the truth of this, I desire to marry her to whom this ring belongs. It is not likely that she who owns so pretty a finger is a rustic or a peasant."

The King and the Queen took the ring, examined it with great curiosity, and agreed with the Prince that it could only belong to the daughter of a good house. Then the King, having embraced his son, and entreated him to get well, went out. He ordered the drums and fifes and trumpets to be sounded throughout the town, and the heralds to cry that she whose finger a certain ring would fit should marry the heir to the throne.

First the Princesses arrived, then the duchesses, and the marquises, and the baronesses; but though they did all they could to make their fingers small, none could put on the ring. So the country girls had to be tried, but pretty though they all were, they all had fingers that were too fat. The Prince, who was feeling better, made the trial himself. At last it was the turn of the chamber-maids; but they succeeded no better. Then, when everyone else had tried, the Prince asked for the kitchen-maids, the scullions, and the sheep-girls. They were all brought to the palace, but their coarse red, short, fingers would hardly go through the golden hoop as far as the nail.

"You have not brought that Donkey-skin, who made me the cake," said the Prince.

Everyone laughed and said, "No," so dirty and unpleasant was she.

"Let someone fetch her at once," said the King; "it shall not be said that I left out the lowliest." And the servants ran laughing and mocking to find the goose-girl.

The Princess, who had heard the drums and the cries of the heralds, had no doubt that the ring was the cause of this uproar. Now, she loved the Prince, and, as true love is timorous and has no vanity, she was in perpetual fear that some other lady would be found to have a finger as small as hers. Great, then, was her joy when the messengers came and knocked at her door. Since she knew that they were seeking the owner of the right finger on which to set her ring, some impulse had moved her to arrange her hair with great care, and to put on her beautiful silver corsage, and the petticoat full of furbelows and silver lace studded with emeralds. At the first knock she quickly covered her finery with the donkey-skin and opened the door. The visitors, in derision, told her that the King had sent for her in order to marry her to his son. Then with loud peals of laughter they led her to the Prince, who was astonished at the garb of this girl, and dared not believe that it was she whom he had seen so majestic and so beautiful. Sad and confounded, he said, " Is it you who lodge at the bottom of that dark alley in the third yard of the farm ? "

" Yes, your Highness," she replied.

" Show me your hand," said the Prince trembling, and heaving a deep sigh.

Imagine how astonished everyone was ! The King and the Queen, the chamberlains and all the courtiers were dumb-founded, when from beneath that black and dirty skin came a delicate little white and rose-pink hand, and the ring slipped without difficulty on to the prettiest little finger in the world. Then, by a little movement which the Princess made, the skin fell from her shoulders and so enchanting was her guise, that the Prince, weak though he was, fell on his knees and held her so closely that she blushed. But that was scarcely noticed, for the King and Queen came to embrace her heartily, and to ask her if she would marry their son. The Princess, confused by all these caresses and by the love of the handsome young Prince, was about to thank them when suddenly the ceiling opened, and the Lilac-fairy descended in a chariot made of the branches and flowers from which she took her name, and, with great charm, told the Princess's story. The King and Queen, overjoyed to know that Donkey-skin was a great Princess redoubled their caresses, but the Prince was even more sensible of her virtue, and his love increased as the Fairy unfolded her tale. His impatience to marry her, indeed, was so great that he could scarcely allow time for the necessary preparations for the grand wedding which was their due. The King and Queen, now entirely devoted to their daughter-in-law, overwhelmed her with affection. She had declared that she could not marry the Prince without the consent of the King her father, so, he was the first to whom an invitation to the wedding was sent; he was not, however, told the name of the bride. The Lilac-fairy, who, as was right, presided over all, had recommended this course to prevent trouble. Kings came from all the countries round, some in sedan-chairs, others in beautiful carriages; those who came from the most distant countries rode on elephants and tigers and eagles. But the most magnificent and most glorious of all was the father of the Princess. He had happily recovered his reason, and had married a Queen who was a widow and very beautiful, but by whom he had no child. The Princess ran to him, and he recognised her at once and embraced her with great tenderness before she had time to throw herself on her knees. The King and Queen presented their son to him, and the happiness of all was complete. The nuptials were celebrated with all imaginable pomp, but the young couple were hardly aware of the ceremony, so wrapped up were they in one another.

In spite of the protests of the noble-hearted young man, the Prince's father caused his son to be crowned the same day, and kissing his hand, placed him on the throne.

The celebrations of this illustrious marriage lasted nearly three months, but the love of the two young people would have endured for more than a hundred years, had they out-lived that age, so great was their affection for one another.

The Moral

It scarce may be believed,
This tale of Donkey-skin;
But laughing children in the home;
Yea, mothers, and grandmothers too,
Are little moved by facts!
By them *'twill be received.*

THE FAIRY TALES OF CHARLES PERRAULT
Printed on 150 gsm Chinese Premium paper 1.3
Bound in Wibalin

DISTRIBUTED BY DOVER PUBLICATIONS, INC.